Chasing the Codex
(A Mystery by 24 Authors)

Cozy Cat Press
Edited by Patricia Rockwell

For information, email **Cozy Cat Press**, cozycatpress@aol.com or visit our website at: www.cozycatpress.com

COZY CAT
P R E S S

ISBN: 978-1939816-79-5

Printed in the United States of America

Cover design by Zoe Shtorm

1 2 3 4 5 6 7 8 9 10

Dear Reader: This book is the 100th title published by Cozy Cat Press. When we published our first cozy mysteries back in 2010, we had no idea our small independent book company would ever get to the point where we could say that we had published 100 books! But we have, and we have you—our readers—to thank for this monumental achievement. Thank you!

This book is a "group mystery." By "group," we mean that it was written by a group of authors, not just one author alone. How did we do this? We gave the parameters of the book to all our authors (a cozy mystery, naturally, with no bad language, grotesque violence, or ribald sex), and then the first author wrote the first chapter. When he was finished, he sent the book to the second author, who wrote the second chapter, and so on and so forth. In the end, we had 24 authors (or pairs of authors) who each wrote a chapter for this book. When the book was complete, our editor Patricia Rockwell, worked with all of the authors to compose a title. We settled on CHASING THE CODEX. Then, to add even more fun, we devised a book cover contest with *99Designs.com* and allowed designers all over the globe the opportunity to create a cover for our book. After all, we figured, if multiple authors wrote the story, a similar number should attempt to design the cover. You can see the winning results on the outside.

This book is dedicated to all of the authors at Cozy Cat Press.

Chapter One
by Christian Belz

Something was missing. It was not as obvious as a gap on a bookshelf, or the small ring of dust where a Royal Doulton figurine had stood. Nothing seemed out of place in the old store, nothing she could name. But the pressure of an unknown void bugged Bryndis Palmer like a pebble in her shoe.

Her first batch of cinnamon cross buns had come out of the oven scorched, and when she'd pulled the tag on a fresh bag of coffee, it had ripped and spilled all over the floor. Her schedule was off even before she'd opened for business. She'd stared at the coffee pot as she wondered what was wrong.

It's nothing. She shook herself out of her stupor, glanced up and looked through the large beveled glass front window of her bookshop The Neglected Word, and smiled at the familiar sight of Tony crossing the street. He stopped at her front door and bent over. *What is he doing?* He straightened up and fumbled to rearrange his backpack. Bryndis caught a flash of red as he came in.

With practiced elegance, Bryndis selected a cup and a saucer from the shelf behind her, and placed them on the counter. Carefully she poured coffee. Tony strode across the wooden floor and held up a brightly wrapped candy-box-sized gift. He offered a bright smile. "Hey, Bryn, this was leaning up against your front door." He handed her the parcel. "It's got your name on it."

Bryndis eyed the package—the glossy red wrapping paper, the black lace ribbon and bow. Agitated, her heart beat faster.

"What's new?" he said, sliding onto a stool at the counter.

"Hmm. Someone left a gift at my door." She glanced up at Tony's intense blue eyes, made more vivid by his indigo sweater. Her apprehension loosened. "I made apple cinnamon cross buns. They're still warm. Want one?" He nodded and she placed one on a plate.

He took a bite. "Wow! This is amazing!"

Bryndis studied the tag dangling from the bow on the package. *This could only mean one thing. And I'm not having it.*

"I know you're dying to open that, but I really need a favor," Tony said. "Can I borrow a copy of Alice Munro's *Vintage Munro*? I need it for second hour."

"This isn't a library, Tony." Bryndis looked at him pointedly. "And the teacher is supposed to remember his supplies. You know, set a good example." She could see the anticipation on his face. Tony was her ex-boyfriend's younger brother and she felt a little protective of him—a feeling which extended as far back as high school when Tony had been just thirteen. She softened. "Should be a copy on one of the shelves in front. When you bring it back, I'll add it to my café counter collection."

"Great, thanks," he said.

Her thoughts returned to the package in her hands. Her knuckles going white as she gripped it harder, she studied her name on the tag, written in bold letters with a black felt-tip pen. The space marked "from" was blank. *Why is he doing this?*

She suddenly scooted sideways through a break in the counter, and barreled toward the far wall which separated her shop from the business next door. "Help yourself to the coffee!" she called over her shoulder to Tony. She yanked open an aluminum and glass door that connected the two stores. "This won't take long!"

She stormed into the neighboring shop, crossing a vinyl tile floor, all the while craning her neck from side to side, and running her eyes along rows of white washing machines and grey dryers. The only people in sight were a woman in her early twenties and a toddler sitting next to her on dilapidated orange plastic chairs. The toddler swung his legs back and forth, his eyes fixed on one of the washers in front of him. Suds behind the glass door churned in circles. The place smelled like soap.

Bryndis's eyes finally settled on the service end of the Laundromat, near the rear of the shop, beneath a sign that advertised "Dry Cleaning." A teen-aged girl was slouched behind the counter, twirling her hair. She jumped when Bryndis slammed the gift-wrapped box down in front of her. "Where is he?"

A whoosh of air and a door shut in the dark void behind her. The girl muttered, "Who? Oh, um, he's—"

"I'm here!" a baritone voice called out from the shadows." A man came into view, hustling quickly toward Bryndis as he peeled off his windbreaker. "You lookin' for me?"

"Stop leaving me gifts, Weston!" Bryndis said with a raised voice. The counter girl slinked off to the side.

The man glanced down at the package and grinned at Bryndis. "Looks like a nice wrap job," he said.

"Come on," she said. "How many times do I need to tell you to leave me alone?" She punctuated her words by stamping her foot, and instantly regretted straining the heel of her Michael Kors boot.

Weston's gleaming head of hair, the color of a Hershey bar, turned toward her as he leaned down to inspect the package. "I'd never buy you chocolates," he said. "Too common." He winked a blue eye at her.

"This isn't from you?"

He spread his arms and shook his head.

How she hated guys leaving little gifts for her. Flowers at her door. A Captain Kirk bobble head on her counter. How quickly she'd jumped to this conclusion––apparently incorrectly this time. At least she was wrong about Weston Blake. Bryndis lowered her head, her rage collapsing as quickly as it had arisen.

"But obviously someone's interested," Weston said. He shuffled through the break in the counter and started toward the front windows of the Laundromat. He said good morning to the woman customer and her son, then paused at a large whiteboard on a side wall, next to a grouping of plastic chairs and a magazine rack.

He picked up a red marker. "What's your special today?" he called back to Bryndis.

Bryndis squared her shoulders and stomped across the floor. She snatched the marker from him. "I'll do it." She looked up at the heading:

THE NEGLECTED WORD
Chalet Shopping Center
Harpshead, MO
SPECIALS

She wrote in neat handwriting *Apple Cinnamon Cross Buns* and *Soup: Mushroom Barley*.

"Why don't you make that three bean soup anymore? It's a taste of heaven."

Bryndis scoffed and choked back her response. In the next moment, she walked out the front door onto the sidewalk, heading away from the Laundromat, taking in the fall air. She stepped back towards her bookshop and paused to shake off the Laundromat exchange. Weston

Blake was basically a nice guy who'd tried too hard to get her attention when she and Holt had broken up. *I have to learn to get along with my neighbors*, she thought. She took a breath and noticed the September sky growing lighter in the distance, turning a vivid pink that deepened her ease.

She'd left Tony sitting at her counter, and she should be returning. She found Tony's demeanor refreshing—so lively and charismatic. As a teenager, he would always get into trouble—step-on-the-neighbor's-daisies kind of trouble, nothing more serious—and would come to her for advice. They'd forged a nice sibling kind of bond while she'd dated his brother Holt for four years. She'd broken up with Holt just before she quit college. That was eight years ago. Two years after that, she and Holt had reunited, until six months prior when they'd broken up for good. Meanwhile, Tony had graduated from Eastern Missouri State University with a BA in English and now with the local public schools barely back in session, he was a busy substitute teacher, on the call sheet at four districts.

Bryndis was taken with the rays of vermilion now streaking across the skyline. *What was that sailor's saying? Red sky at morning?* As her eyes drifted down to the eastern horizon in the direction of St. Louis, she noticed a large group of women in tights and Reeboks, standing restlessly in front of the shop on the other side of hers—Furst Training. The group included Betty Jo Kramer, her thunder thighs in purple tights, strutting around practically screaming: *Here I am, guys!* Bryndis could make out her cellulite through the Spandex.

She turned to enter her shop. The bell jangled as she pulled open the door. From the corner of her eye, Bryndis caught purple moving behind her. *Oh, no, here she comes!* Her respect for Betty Jo had dissolved eight years earlier. They'd been at Missouri State together, where Betty Jo had roomed with Bryndis's best friend, Claire, who'd constantly relayed to Bryndis stories of Betty Jo's nasty personal habits. Claire had told her how Betty Jo would pull an ice cream container out of the freezer, scrape ice cream out with her fingers, pop it into her mouth, then return the container back to the fridge. That was before Bryndis gave up on college altogether during her fourth semester and started working at this bookstore. Her Aunt Snaedis had gotten her the job—as she was good friends with the owner of the Chalet Shopping Mall and proprietor of The Neglected Word, Elena Vasquez. Having found her passion at The Neglected Word and a soul mate in her new boss, Elena, Bryndis was, in short order, promoted to assistant manager, then manager. When Elena had retired the year before, Bryndis had bought the place. She loved her shop and having her elderly aunt just two doors down from her.

"Bryn! Bryn!" Betty Jo called after her.

Bryndis threw the woman a glance as she slid in behind the counter. Realizing she was still holding the wrapped package, she quickly tossed it into the waste can on top of the morning's scorched pastries and coffee grounds. To Tony she said, "More coffee?" He nodded. She grabbed the pot and refilled his cup.

Betty Jo, who was only five feet two, pushed up to the counter beside Tony, huffing and puffing, and leaned in, setting her ample breasts on the Corian counter top. "Hey, where's your boyfriend?" she said to Bryndis. "He's late for our aerobicize class."

Bryndis slid a pile of display books down the counter, away from Betty Jo's elbows. She liked to keep books on the counter for her customers to read over coffee and pastries. She would later sell these "counter books" at a discount. *The Battered Smile* was on top of the pile.

"Not my boyfriend." She glanced at Tony. "My ex."

Betty Jo said, "Oh really? He didn't say anything about breaking up with.... Oh, whatever. He's late and we're all standing out there waiting. I need to get to work. I only took this class because all my best friends were taking it. That way, we can catch up on the week's happenings—"

Bryndis cut her off. "He must have overslept again." To Tony she said, "Your brother needs to learn some responsibility."

Tony grinned and turned his palms up—*what do you want me to do?*

Another confrontation with Holt was the last thing Bryndis needed, especially after last night's argument. Holt could be assertive, and when he went overboard—like he had last night—it had a way of getting her ire up and that wasn't good for anyone. She paused, feeling the glare from Betty Jo. "You have a seat. I'll go check on him." She tapped her finger on the glass pastry bell jar. "A cinnamon cross bun while you wait? Fresh this morning."

With a huff, Betty Jo said sure, with coffee, and mounted a stool. "So, is he seeing anyone?"

Bryndis pulled out a plate, grabbed the tongs, and put a pastry on a dish. *Might as well just tape these on your hips.* "I wouldn't know, Betty Jo." She turned to pick up the coffee pot and glanced at the wall-long mirror. A sticky note caught her eye: "Frida. St. Louis Airport. Thursday, 3:00 p.m." With alarm, she realized that today was Thursday. She wasn't prepared for Frida's visit—at least, not mentally. She rested her hip against the back counter. She still needed to pack, but she'd secured their room reservations at the convention hotel in St. Louis. She was looking forward to the book convention, but having her fourteen-year-old niece along meant more work for her. Finding things to do.

Making sure her meals were nutritious. Worrying about Frida getting lost. Should she censor what the girl saw? What breakout sessions she attended? But maybe it would be fun. After all, she always had a blast with her sister Lia and her kids when she visited them in Santa Barbara. Like when they'd all gone hiking. The breathtaking views of the ocean! But this was different. She would have *responsibility*.

Three days at the Midwest Book Lovers' Convention, viewing exhibits and attending workshops about classic novels, modern romance books, crime fiction—well, anything and everything book related—would certainly give them both something to do. It would surely entertain the book-loving Frida for a few days. Aunt Snædis had promised to look after her bookstore while she and Frida were away. Snaedis would just put up a sign on the door of her dress shop, Modiste, two doors down at the small Chalet Shopping Center, and handle both businesses from the book shop.

Bryndis poured Betty Jo a cup of coffee. To Tony, she said, "I need you to go with me. This is the second time this month. Maybe you can talk some sense into him."

"Sure." Tony checked his watch and gulped the last of his coffee. "Then I have to run. Class is in thirty minutes. School's barely started and I don't want to set a bad example so early in the year."

It cracked her up to see Tony's maturity. Not too long ago, he'd been a kid himself. But she was glad he enjoyed his work. With her heels clicking on the wooden floor, Bryndis led the way through the back of her store, past rows of bookshelves, through the door marked "EMPLOYEES ONLY" to the storage room where boxes of new arrivals for Mother's Day—still many months away—awaited unpacking. She thought with happiness about the books she'd selected, titles she'd enjoy herself. A few had been recommended by her own mother and her friends. She'd kept copious notes about what they liked.

At the back of the storage room was a solid metal door with a peephole which she never looked through during the daytime. She unlocked it and tugged the door open. The morning air was refreshing, with a slight smell of pine.

"Hey," she said, turning to Tony who was immediately behind her. "I've been meaning to mention your Facebook page. I really love the little snippets of conversation with the students in your classes that you put in your status updates. Do you really rap? They must think you're so awesome."

Tony stopped and struck a "hip" pose:

"Follow my logic, stop playing the tunes.
You've spent the minutes to be in school.
Some folks like Longfellow, Carroll, Thoreau.
Ruminate, cogitate, please don't be bogue.
Follow your passion,
No need to ration.
You could move to the mansion.
You may not waltz like the Viennese.
You may not want to learn Archimedes.
But for me, numbers are a disease."

Bryndis laughed.

"Ah, kids are cool," sighed Tony.

"How do you get so lucky? Seems they all enjoy having you."

"Ah, they're great—mostly. Only one or two troublemakers."

They continued out the back door, turned to the right, past the Laundromat, to an old wooden staircase which accessed a continuous balcony along the second story of the small strip mall, from which the apartments above the stores could be reached. There was a stairway at each end. Weston Blake's Laundromat, Bryndis's bookstore The Neglected Word, Holt's gym Furst Fitness, and her Aunt Snædis's dress shop Modiste at the far end each had apartments above. From behind, the entire brick building resembled a quaint farm structure like something out of *Gone With the Wind.* For all Bryndis knew, the original Chalet Shopping Center could have been a barn or workers' quarters on a farm back in the mid-1800s. All she knew for sure from discussions with her previous boss and mentor, Elena, was that the structure had undergone numerous redesigns and refurbishing until it had reached its present eclectic look. Her bookshop was a double-wide store and had two smaller apartments above it, with the second one in between Bryndis's place and Holt's apartment. This was a blessing after they'd broken up, because she didn't want to hear him making noises in his apartment all the time. They'd taken on the practice of parking at opposite ends of the building too.

Bryndis thought about what she would say. *Or should I leave the whole thing to Tony?* Not only was it rude for Holt to leave paying customers at his gym door, but most of the women standing there had jobs to get to. If he kept this up, his customer base would evaporate. Maybe he just needed better technology to wake him. Setting two alarms would be good. Even one. But she knew Holt prided himself on waking up naturally. His body was *in tune,* he often said. This quality had originally attracted her to him—not the lack of an alarm clock, but his free-spirited nature.

The phone in her pocket rang—Janet Jackson's *Escapade*—and she answered as she stopped on the balcony.

"Hi, Aunt Bryn! I'm at the airport in Los Angeles and I'll be getting on the plane in a few minutes."

"Oh, hi, sweetheart," Bryndis said to her young niece Frida. "You have a nice flight, and I'll see you this afternoon. Did you get a window seat?"

"Uh-huh, and it's in front of the wing, so I'll be able to see down on top of the clouds. It will be magical."

"And you can tell me all about it when you get here," she said and chuckled warmly. They said goodbye and Bryndis's thoughts turned back to Holt. Last night he'd been standing outside his apartment when she'd come upstairs after closing her store— staring at his door. When she'd asked if something was wrong, he'd snapped at her. *No.*

"Lost your key?" she'd asked.

"It's here somewhere."

"Maybe you left it in your car," she'd said.

"Just go on home, Bryn. Don't worry about it. I forgot to get the mail anyway." And he'd walked back down the stairs to the mailboxes. When they'd been together, they would retrieve their mail together hand in hand. Now they didn't even speak much. She'd watched him take some letters out of the box, then walk over to his car and open the back door. Maybe he'd left the keys down there. Wouldn't have been the first time. He'd been forgetful about a lot of things lately. Rather than watch him further, she'd gone inside her place. A short while later, she'd heard his footsteps on the balcony, and then his door slamming. When she'd gone out to look, his kitchen light was on.

Now she stood in front of his place with Tony.

Ceiko was at Holt's door. *Meew! Meew!*

"Hey, she shouldn't be out here," Bryndis said, picking up the cat.

"I'll knock," Tony said and pounded on the door. "Holt! Open up. Holt!"

Bryndis peeked over the filigreed wooden railing at the parking lot. Holt's black Charger was in its usual parking spot, where it had been last night, next to a slab of grass scattered with morning glories that were climbing a fence behind the picnic table. *Oh, the early mornings we sat out there at that table, not too long ago, lingering over coffee and kisses.*

She peered into Holt's kitchen window and gasped. "We gotta get in there!" She bent down, pulled up a piece of loose wood trim by the door frame and retrieved a key.

Tony was already pushing in the door. "Don't bother; it's unlocked." They hesitated in the doorway at the sight before them. Two wooden kitchen chairs were on their side; mail was strewn about the floor. A small table was askew, with at least a couple of drinking glasses on the floor, broken. A kitchen trash can was on its side, with coffee grounds, microwave dinner boxes, and used paper towels scattered about.

"Holt!" she called, her heart thumping in her chest.

Tony made his way across the floor to the living room, Bryndis following. "My God! What happened here?" he said.

Couch cushions were tossed about. Papers and books littered the floor. A bookcase was bare, except for a few books lying on their sides at uncommon angles. Bryndis trod through the mess toward the bedroom, her pulse racing. The bedroom door was open a crack. She pushed in. The metal bed frame was intact. The mattress was leaning against the wall. No Holt.

Bryndis pulled out her phone. Punched in Holt's number. Music sounded by the bedroom window. *We will. We will. Rock you.*

"That's his phone!" Tony said.

She moved over to the window, bent down and picked up the cellphone. Stared at it.

"Call 911," she whispered hoarsely.

Chapter Two
by Lane Buckman

Frida shifted in her seat. She was excited. *Dreadfully excited*, she thought. *Dreadfully excited* sounded more like how her favorite heroine would feel embarking on her first flight. Average people were excited. Jane Eyre would be dreadfully excited. Jane Eyre would tuck her seatbelt in with efficiency, then study the plane's interior with her sharp, intelligent eyes and think deep, serious thoughts about how amazing it all was.

So, Frida pulled her journal from the knapsack tucked carefully under the seat in front of her, and gave her attention to writing deep, serious thoughts. She was so focused on composing a description of the seatback tray that she nearly missed her very first takeoff, but once she found herself leaning backwards with the ground falling away at a neat angle—her stomach going with it, Frida forgot her journal altogether.

She was traveling to see her aunt Bryndis, who lived in what Frida's mother called a "delightful, antique-filled apartment above her charming, bric-a-brac-filled bookstore, in a pleasing antique shopping strip, on an appealing street, in a warm, inviting, sleepy little town south of St. Louis." It sounded very different from Frida's bustling home, filled with her brothers' sweat socks and soccer gear, carpool lines, and kids whose main interests were killing off aliens in video games, or memorizing the alliterative offspring of Hollywood royalty. To Frida, a charming old bookstore sounded like heaven.

Frida wasn't sure exactly how it had come to pass, but her mother had told Aunt Bryndis that Frida was suffering from some unknown teenage malaise. Aunt Bryndis had come up with the idea of the two of them going on a trip together to a book convention in St. Louis, as the event occurred in early September shortly before Frida was expected to return to school. "Maybe you'll meet some of your *people* there," Frida's mother, Lia, had said. "And you can make FaceFriends with them."

"*Facebook*, Mom," Frida had corrected. "And I don't really do that computer thing. You know that."

"Which is why Aunt Bryndis is taking you to a place where humans of your ilk might meet up. Other bookworms, that is. Just behave. And be nice."

Behaving Frida could do. *Nice* was a little more difficult. Nice meant something different to everyone, it seemed. To her mother, *nice* meant quiet. *Be quiet and don't cause a bother.* Her mother had enough bother with her sons—without her daughter causing a ruckus. To Frida's brothers, *nice* meant staying out of their way, their rooms, and their backyard games. To her father, *nice* meant staying away from boys. To the boys at school, *nice* meant something of which her father would certainly disapprove. To the girls at school, *nice* meant Jane Austen—not Jane Eyre—as Frida was fairly certain Jane Eyre wouldn't have been at all interested in Austen's Mark Darcy.

Frida had plenty of time to consider the differences in Janes, so much so that by the time her flight landed in St. Louis, she'd made quite a dent in her forehead, having fallen asleep against the rim of the airplane's window. She had a groggy moment of disconnect, then scrambled to retrieve her journal and pen and stuff them back into her knapsack before joining the hurry-up-and-wait queue to exit the plane.

"Buh-bye. Bye now. Buh-bye," a flight attendant said, waving the weary string of passengers along. She grinned broadly at Frida when she approached the front. "Did you enjoy your flight?"

Frida nodded. "I did. Thanks."

"Do you know where to go from here?"

"Baggage? G-6?"

"Exactly!" The attendant gave a brief, cheery list of directions, and sent her on her way with a genuine, "Have a great time on your trip."

Frida exited into the Hoover-attachment-looking tube that carried her onto the concourse and into a microcosm of humanity. She stood still for a moment watching mothers wrestle bags and babies through throngs of businessmen and young adults wearing backpacks, and well-heeled women dressed for a very different kind of runway, and kids like herself. No wonder her mother had given up travel when her brothers were young.

It was like life passing before her eyes, and she wished she could write and walk at the same time because she was having some seriously deep thoughts she didn't want to forget. It was almost enough to make her wish she'd let her mother get her that cell phone with all the features, but Frida highly doubted that Jane Eyre would ever carry a cell phone, so she'd asked for the Moleskine journal instead. For a second, she even wished she'd taken her mother up on the offer to borrow *her* phone for the trip, but once she'd called her aunt before going through security, she hadn't seen the point in it.

It took no time to get to the baggage claim. Since she'd known she was coming, Frida had been studying the airport maps. The last thing she wanted was to look like someone's lost child, and she was proud to have managed her way to G-6 with only a few backward glances. Her co-passengers reassembled themselves from having scattered after the flight, in ones, twos, and clumps of family and friends—all waiting for their belongings to rise up out of the carousel.

Frida counted, and her bag came up tenth in line. "You'll appreciate it later," her mother had promised, tying on a garish pink and lime green bow that would differentiate her black bag from everyone else's. Grudgingly, Frida agreed, having just watched two ladies arguing over a zebra-striped case.

Now, with her suitcase in hand, all that was left to do was find Aunt Bryndis. Once more, Frida told herself, *I am dreadfully excited!*

Aunt Bryndis had promised to meet her at the arrivals area of G-6, which seemed easy enough. So, she squared her shoulders, hoisted up her suitcase and strode toward the sliding doors that would take her to her aunt and an even greater adventure.

She paused as she passed a gaggle of men wearing suits and chauffeur caps, each holding a sign with a name. *Frida Bonita,* one sign read. She was bumped along by the person behind her, who hadn't expected her to stop, then turned around after apologizing. *Frida Bonita* was Aunt Bryndis's nickname for her.

"Miss Bonita?" asked the driver holding the sign with her nickname.

"Uhm...." Frida looked around for anyone else who might go by that name. Plenty of women were hurrying past. Any one of them might be named Frida Bonita, she guessed. Likelier, they were named Melissa, or Denise, or Amy, but maybe someone else was Frida.

"Frida Flynn?" The driver flipped his sign over. Three flips. Frida Flynn to Frida Bonita. Frida Bonita to Frida Flynn. Frida Flynn back to Frida Bonita.

That was certainly her name. She said so, and the driver smiled. "Your aunt sent me to retrieve you."

He punctuated his English accent with a little bow and offered his arm. Frida and the other drivers eyed him warily. *Who does that?*

He wagged his eyebrows. "Come along, Miss Flynn. Your aunt was detained at her shop, and she's asked me to bring you to her there."

"I… Uhm…" Frida stammered, flipping through the card catalog in her brain, thinking perhaps she should upgrade to a super computer after all. *What would Jane Eyre do?*

She lifted her chin. "Did my aunt tell you the password?"

"Your nickname is the password." He smiled.

Frida frowned. There was no password.

"There is no password." The driver seemed to read her face. "But your aunt said you'd recognize your nickname paired with your name. Frida Bonita." He held up the sign and flipped it once more. "Frida Flynn."

"And you're going to take me to her shop?"

"The very same. Yes."

"I just wasn't expecting this."

"No, of course not. Would you like to phone her, or send her a text message?"

Frida bit at her lips. "I don't have a cell phone."

The driver seemed to take this information in stride, and merely shrugged. "I could lend you mine."

"That's okay. I mean—you know my nickname." And he had very nice brown eyes.

"Come along then. Your aunt will be thinking I've absconded with you."

Frida chuckled, the spark of excitement that her confusion had dampened fanned back to life at the thought of being driven by an actual chauffeur. "I'm Elwin, by the way," the driver told her, reaching for her suitcase. "An old friend of your aunt's."

"Frida," she pointed to herself. "But I guess you knew that."

"It's what the sign says." Elwin offered another smile full of crooked teeth.

He led her out of the foot traffic of the airport and down the sidewalk to the biggest, shiniest limousine she'd ever seen. When he opened the back door for her, she slid inside, wondering what the people walking past made of it. Did they wonder if she was a child star? Did they think she was the scion to an internet fortune? A hotel heiress? Some foreign diplomat's daughter?

"Dreadfully exciting," she whispered, hugging herself as the lid of the limousine trunk closed down on her tackily be-ribboned suitcase.

Elwin took his place behind the steering wheel, looking back through the open window space between the front and back seats. "Hungry? Want something to drink?"

"I—yeah," Frida nodded, the idea of having a meal in a limo suddenly appealing.

"There's a mini-bar there," Elwin said and pointed out with a wink. "No alcohol, though. You'll find snacks as well."

"Thank you!"

"No worries." And with that, Elwin pressed a button that raised a black screen between them, obscuring him from view.

The door locks clicked as the engine came to life, and Frida spent a few happy minutes working her way through the mini-bar and snacks. Curiosity and growling stomach sated, she shifted to the far side of the back bench seat to try out its view, pressing her forehead to the glass to peer at the cars passing by. With windows tinted so black, no one could see her. She felt like a spy, or at least someone very important.

After a while, she bounced to the seat facing her, then worked her way around all the seating options until she'd come back to where she'd first situated herself and her knapsack. This was definitely worth a journal entry, and she'd written a few hundred words before it occurred to her to wonder how long it should have taken to get from the airport to her aunt's shop.

According to the map she'd consulted ahead of time, it was about eighty miles from the airport terminal to Aunt Bryn's bookshop, The Neglected Word. If they were traveling at sixty miles per hour, accounting for how long it might take to get out of the airport itself, traffic, and anything else that might slow them down, she'd figured for ninety minutes. Granted, she'd assumed Aunt Bryndis would be collecting her—not Elwin, certainly not a limousine.

According to her watch, she'd been on the ground for an hour and a half. She hadn't looked to see what time it was when they'd started driving, but she thought it must have been at least an hour. *So a half hour more, at most,* she thought.

Forty minutes later, when the car had not so much as slowed, Frida tapped on the privacy glass. Static crackled and Elwin's voice filled the backseat. "Yes, ma'am?"

"I, oh! Intercom. I was wondering how long it would be until we got to my aunt's?"

"Not long now," Elwin promised.

"Are we close?"

The static sound had gone, and Frida wondered if that meant Elwin hadn't heard her question. She tapped on the glass again.

"Yes, ma'am?"

"I'm sorry—are we close?"

"We are. Yes. No worries. Just relax and enjoy your ride."

"We are going to The Neglected Word, right? At the Chalet Shopping Center? On Congress? In Harpshead?"

"Of course, darling," Elwin comforted her. "Of course. The Neglected Word. Chalet. Congress. Harpshead. Of course."

Frida frowned. Something felt wrong. But this was her aunt's friend, who knew her special nickname as well as her real name, who'd come to pick her up because her aunt was delayed, and her aunt wouldn't have wanted her to worry. She tapped on the glass again.

This time Elwin sounded frustrated. "Yes?"

"Can you take the privacy glass down?"

"No. I'm sorry."

"Why not?"

"Driving distraction. Road rules. Doctor's orders and all that."

The intercom went dead again. Frida hesitated, then tapped again. No answer. So she knocked at the window. Then she pounded at the window. Then she slapped her flat palms against the partition, yelling for Elwin to answer her. The responding silence was terrifying. Her dreadful excitement turned to dread.

She fell back into the bench seat and stared at the partition, willing it to open and willing herself not to cry. Neither did the least amount of good. There was always the chance, she told herself, that Elwin just didn't like teens, or children, or people of any age who asked, "Are we there yet?" But, there was also a chance that something awful had happened to her aunt, and this man was part of it. If something had happened to Aunt Bryndis, who was going to come to her rescue so far away from home? She didn't even have a cell phone. She had fleeting unkind thoughts about what Jane Eyre might do, and imagined Jane Eyre having them right back. After all, Jane was a modern woman for her time, and wouldn't have eschewed technology for the sheer romance of it. But she'd need to think about that later. A paradigm shift was going to have to wait. Right now, Frida was sure she was being kidnapped.

"Be smart, Frida," she told herself. "Be your own hero."

What tools did she have? She'd already tried to roll down the windows. Finding them locked only furthered her fears. She had a pen and paper. She had three books, clean underwear and socks, all the regular toiletries, and a small stuffed bear in her knapsack.

As usual, she went back to pen and paper, scrawling notes which she folded and stuffed into the mini-bar, the snack wall, under the floor mats and between the seats. She'd just tucked away the twentieth note when she felt the car beginning to slow. It was a long shot, but maybe the next passenger, or the person who would clean the car, or someone—anyone—would find the white corners she'd left peeking out of their hiding places.

She imagined someone unfolding a note and reading, "September 2. My name is Frida Fellows Flynn. I've been kidnapped by a man named Elwin. He is tall and thin, with crooked teeth and brown eyes. He has an English accent. Please contact my parents and my aunt." She hoped the reader would be able to make out the addresses and phone numbers she'd copied so hastily.

Frida had just finished tucking her journal and pen back into her knapsack when the car rolled to a stop. She was trying to decide whether to try to bolt and make a run for it, or huddle in the corner away from any prying hands when the door flew open and a body was shoved inside.

Before she could react, the door was shut and locked again, and even before the man had righted himself, the car was moving forward. Frida scrambled as far back from the newcomer as possible, truly afraid for her life.

As the man found footing enough to pull himself up onto the seat facing her, she got a good look at him. He was disheveled and bloodied, his shirt torn and wrinkled, his nose far off center from what she remembered. And that made her realize she'd seen him before.

He propped himself up against the side of the car with a grunt, reaching to touch his swollen face, and that was when a name came to Frida's mind. A name that connected him to her aunt, a name she'd heard her mother asking after over the phone, a name Aunt Bryndis had used more than once when she'd visited them.

It was Aunt Bryndis's boyfriend, Holt.

Chapter Three
by Sally Carpenter

"Bryn! There's somebody at the door!" Tony's voice wafted through the apartment to where Bryndis stood—shell shocked—in her ex-boyfriend's bedroom.

"Police?" she called back. She couldn't imagine the cops arriving so quickly to Tony's 911 call.

"No. Somebody's looking for my brother."

Bryndis tucked Holt's cell phone into her pants' pocket and returned to the disheveled living room. On the balcony, just outside the open door, stood a man who apparently had arrived via a time loop straight from Woodstock. A bandana held back his long, stringy hair. His face sported acne scars and a Van Dyke beard. He wore a long-sleeved tie-dyed t-shirt, a fringed leather vest, faded jeans and leather sandals. The smell of musky incense clung to his clothes. Ceiko, wary of strangers, scooted beneath the sofa.

The intruder smiled at Bryndis. He spoke in a soft, melodious voice. "Hey, chickie, what's new? Where's Holt?"

Her eyes flashed. "I'm not your chickie. My name is Bryndis Palmer. Who are you and what do you want with Holt?"

He held up his hands, palms out. "Hey, cool it, babe—I mean, Bryndis. No harm meant; no harm done. Cats call me Rambler. I'm an old friend of Holt's."

She put her hands on her hips. "Really? I'm an old girlfriend of Holt's and he's never mentioned you. Tony, do you know this man?"

Tony shook his head. "No, he's a stranger to me."

Rambler moved inside the apartment and scanned the room's wreckage. "Hey, what happened here? Did Holt throw a party last night? Must have been a gasser."

"He's missing." She snapped the words.

"Oh, that's a drag. Well, then, I better split. If Holt shows up, tell him the Rambler's gotta see him—PDQ."

He turned to leave but Bryndis quickly slipped around him and stood in the doorway. She stretched out her arms and grabbed both sides of the doorframe to block his exit. "What's your business with Holt? What do you want from him?"

He grinned. His voice fell into a paternalistic singsong. "Don't you worry your pretty little head about that, missy. That's none of your beeswax."

She noticed he held a book-shaped package wrapped in white paper. "What's that in your hand? Is that for Holt?"

The aged flower child stepped back and hid the parcel behind his back. "It's nothing. Nothing at all."

Tony made a grab for the package, but Rambler dodged and gripped the kid's wrist. With a deft martial art throw, he flipped Tony and the kid crashed against the bookcase.

"Tony!" Distracted, Bryndis moved toward her friend. With the door unguarded, Rambler rushed outside. She reached out to stop him, but only succeeded in grabbing his colorful sleeve. The flimsy fabric tore easily, leaving a scrap of clothing in her hand as the stranger escaped.

Bryndis dashed out the door. Rambler sprinted down the balcony to the stairs, his sandals slapping against the wooden flooring. She ran along the balcony in pursuit. Being younger and lighter, she soon gained on him. Only a few feet ahead, Rambler glanced over his shoulder at her. He stopped suddenly, gripped the balcony railing, and vaulted over.

Bryndis skidded to a halt and peered over the edge. The man had landed none too gracefully atop a clump of shrubbery. He scrambled off the bush, jumped onto a vintage motorcycle parked nearby, and started it up. Frustrated and unwilling to likewise somersault off the second floor, Bryndis watched him drive off. She strained to catch a glimpse of the bike's license number but the plate was too small to read at that distance.

When she got back inside Holt's apartment, she kicked at a pile of papers on the floor.

"Don't move anything," Tony said. "The police will want to look at that."

"The place is a shambles. What are they going to learn from this mess?" Bryndis reached down and pulled Tony to his feet. "Are you all right?"

"Nothing broken, just a little shaken. So I guess the nutcase outran you?"

"Apparently." She glanced at the piece of torn cloth in her hand and absently shoved it into her pants' pocket. "Where are the police? They should be here by now. The station isn't that far away."

"Sorry, Bryn. The guy showed up at the door before I could phone."

She sighed. *How could this day get any worse?* "Never mind. I'll call. Shouldn't you be on your way to the school?"

"I hate to leave you alone to deal with the police and all this." Tony gestured around the room.

"I'll be fine as long as no more of Holt's 'old friends',"—she made quote marks in the air with her index fingers—"show up."

"Okay, Bryn, but I really hate leaving you alone. . ."

With the coast apparently clear, Ceiko crawled out from beneath the couch, meowed pitifully, and rubbed against Tony's ankles. He scooped up and cuddled the feline. "Poor Ceiko must have been out all night. I'll take care of her before I go. Come on, cutie; let's get you fed. I think the cat food's in the fridge."

He retreated into the kitchen to find the food and a bowl. Meanwhile, Bryndis began picking up and reshelving the books. She couldn't stand to see books thrown about like discards. At least, she could put away the books before the police arrived.

From the next room, Tony called out, "When the cops get here, be sure to tell them about Rambler. Maybe they can pick him up."

"For what? The police can't arrest someone just because they look like a Deadhead. He didn't do anything illegal. And that package he has—maybe it's something harmless." Although a twist in her gut told her otherwise.

From the kitchen came sounds of a spoon scraping a metal can and the cries of a hungry cat. "Okay, Ceiko, I'm almost ready." A metal bowl hit the hardwood floor.

Bryndis picked up a particular hardback book with a square of neon green paper sticking out from the pages like a bookmark. The paper fell out as she replaced the volume on the shelf. Picking up the scrap, she read the handwritten scrawl: "GO EXPO BTH 153."

Tony left the kitchen. "That should keep the diva happy for a while."

"Tony, does this mean anything to you?" She handed him the paper.

He read it and shook his head. "Looks like Holt's handwriting but I can't tell what it's supposed to mean. He was always writing cryptic notes about errands he needed to run. Say, Bryn, if you need to get back to your shop, why don't I stay here until the police arrive? I'm not scheduled to teach first hour."

The police! With all the craziness going on, she'd forgotten to call. Out of habit, she dug into her pants' pocket for her phone, only to pull out Holt's cell instead. "Hey, Tony."

"Yeah?"

"Do you know the password to your brother's phone or computer?"

"No. Why?"

"If that Rambler guy *is* an old friend, as he says, maybe Holt has a picture of him somewhere."

* * * * *

The man known as Shadow dug through the papers piled on the desk, his generally cool demeanor beginning to crack. Normally, he'd be finished with the job by now. Quick in, get the information, and out. This job was taking too long and had become too messy. Usually, the target told him right away what he needed to know. This target wouldn't talk no matter how much persuasion he'd used. Now the target lay on the apartment's beige wall-to-wall carpet with a bullet hole in his head. That would cost Shadow plenty. His clients didn't pay him to leave bodies behind. That made the police too curious.

Shadow rummaged through the target's desk drawers and pulled out a folded newspaper. Holding the paper in his hands, which were encased in surgical gloves, he spotted an article circled with thick red ink strokes—"Midwest Book Lovers' Convention." Red arrows pointed to the notice. Why would the target care about a bunch of books or the people who loved them? The target didn't seem like the type of guy who read books for fun. When it came to recreational reading, the target probably had the same tastes as Shadow—racing forms and *TV Guide*. He poked around in the drawer some more and found two glossy paper brochures, one about the "Midwest Book Lovers' Convention" and the other describing the convention hotel.

Perhaps this was where Shadow needed to go to find what his client wanted.

He closed the desk drawer and placed the paper items into his briefcase, next to his gun and silencer. He stepped over to the body. His shoes, encased in plastic booties, left no traces of incriminating mud or hairs. From the outside hallway, Shadow heard footsteps. He froze. People stood near the door, laughing and talking. Sounded like they were just returning from an all-night bender. A key scraped the lock. Shadow took a silent step toward his briefcase and reached for the gun.

"Ooops, wrong apartment," one of the voices said. "These doors look alike."

The footsteps moved off and the voices faded as the people moved down the corridor. Shadow knelt beside the body. He removed a ruby ring from the target's finger and the cash from his wallet. As with previous gigs, this would give the impression that the crime had been associated with a robbery and might possibly throw the heat off the track. Shadow prowled the apartment, taking a couple of small ivory figurines that looked valuable. He'd later chuck them into a trash bin. He stuffed the ring, money, and knick-knacks into his briefcase. He set the lock on the satchel and made a quick detour into the bathroom to check his appearance before he left.

In the bathroom, Shadow watched his image in the mirror as he fashioned his top collar button and retied his tie. He ran the tap, tore off some sheets of toilet paper, and wiped a spot of the target's blood from his cheek. After he flushed the bloody paper down the toilet, he smoothed his thick, wavy hair with his pocket comb. Good. Now he looked like a regular businessman on his way to work. As Shadow studied his reflection, he wondered if he still resembled his twin brother, Holt. *Whatever became of him?* he wondered.

Chapter Four
by Barbara Jean Coast

"She's gone?"

Bryndis was left gobsmacked when she arrived at the St. Louis airport's G-6 baggage claim center at 3:30 p.m. In disbelief at the attendant's words, Bryndis thought she was going to pass out. She blindly gazed around, looking for her niece, not seeing anyone who remotely resembled Frida.

The Flyways Airlines' attendant consulted her computer, confirming what she'd already told Bryndis. "The flight got in on time, and according to the schedule, it landed and the passengers departed without incident." She scrolled down the screen again. "Oh."

"What? What *oh*?" Bryndis jumped at the attendant––Wendy, according to her nametag—urging her to continue.

"Well, it's just that there was one person—a woman—who's reporting a missing bag." She paused as she continued to work through the information. "A Mrs. Elsie Turner. She's probably still here, filing a claim."

"Where would she be?"

"At the office, just behind the carousel."

"Thanks." Bryndis made a hasty retreat to G-6 and immediately saw a rather boisterous woman, dressed in floral capris a size or two too small, with hair an unnatural shade of orange.

"That's right—zebra striped." The woman crossed her arms over her ample bosom. "Like I said, just like that other one, but that one wasn't mine."

"What other one, Mrs. Turner?" asked a rather bored-looking male Flyways employee who was taking notes, not bothering to look up at the woman.

Elsie Turner sighed. "The one that other woman left with—obviously not mine, as it was just a cheap knock off."

"You mean the suitcase you damaged?" the attendant confirmed as he flipped back through the notes on his clipboard.

"The one that fell apart," Elsie reiterated. "As I said, it was cheap."

Bryndis interrupted. "Excuse me, have either of you seen this girl?" She brought her phone up to their faces, displaying a recent image of Frida.

They both paused as if considering her question. The employee put his head back down, but Elsie took the device from Bryndis and tilted it to get a better look. "Yes, I believe so," she replied as she gave the phone back to Bryndis.

"When? Is she here?"

Elsie shook her head. "She left, a while ago."

"Left? How?"

"A driver picked her up. With a limo, I think."

"What do you mean?" Bryndis was beyond puzzled.

"A man in a suit with a cap. Had a sign for her, with a funny name—*Frida Banana*—or something. I don't know."

Bryndis's heart was in her throat. She could barely get the word out. "*Bonita?*"

Elsie shrugged, then brightened. "Yeah, that's it."

Bryndis desperately grabbed Elsie's sleeve. "She's my niece and this was her first flight. I was supposed to pick her up, but I was late. No one else was supposed to get her, do you understand?"

Elsie patted her arm. "Listen, honey, that's all I know and I have to get going. I do remember her leaving though—right out those doors." She pointed and then gently lifted Bryndis's arm off of hers and added, "The airline has my name and number. I honestly don't remember seeing anything else, but if they need me, they can reach me at my daughter's house over the next week. Tell them to bring my missing luggage while they're at it." She gave the Flyways' employee a sneer and turned on her heel, heading through the automatic doors to catch a taxi.

A woman in a polyester navy blazer and tan skirt—the airport security uniform—approached Bryndis and the attendant. She introduced herself as Erica Morgan and asked if she could be of any assistance. Bryndis did her best to explain the situation to her, but her words were panicked and muddled. "That's the second person who's disappeared on me today," mumbled Bryndis.

The security woman paused, trying to make sense of what she'd heard. "There's a second missing person from the airport?"

"No." Bryndis shook her head. "Holt Furst, from Harpshead. He is—well, was—my boyfriend. Um, neighbor, acquaintance now, I guess." She rubbed her hands on her jeans nervously, looking around to see if it was possible that Elsie Turner had been mistaken and that Frida would suddenly emerge from the women's restroom.

Agent Morgan studied Bryndis and pursed her lips, trying to read her face. "Why don't you come with me? We'll get you settled down while we start looking for your niece." She waved to another security officer. They ushered Bryndis into a private room and told her to wait there while they called the local police and started their own internal search. They asked her to email Frida's image to their main security address and informed her that they'd circulate a printed version throughout the building, on the off chance that Frida had not actually left as Elsie Turner had claimed to have seen. They would also page her on the PA system. "You mentioned that someone else was missing?" Agent Morgan asked. Bryndis nodded and repeated Holt's name.

The agent waited patiently, giving Bryndis the chance to elaborate on what she'd said. Bryndis shrugged, responding with a brief recap of Holt's disappearance earlier that day and why she'd been late to the airport to pick up Frida. Agent Morgan nodded. She took out a notepad and pen from her inside pocket and placed them on the desktop. "I'll see what I can find out about what happened here. Why don't you write down everything you can remember from this morning on—anything that comes to mind, even if it's small, or you think it's irrelevant. Record it all down."

Bryndis was incredulous. "Do you think their disappearances are related?"

Agent Morgan shrugged as she got up. "More importantly, do *you* think they're related? Any information may help." The security agent and her silent co-worker then left and Bryndis was alone in the sterile room, with just the faint buzz of overhead lights and blank notepad pages to keep her company while she waited. It was excruciating. She couldn't believe that she'd been late for Frida's first flight, or that her niece would be so naïve as to get into a car with a stranger. But then again, who would know about *Frida Bonita*, other than a close family member? Poor girl— what was happening to her? She certainly didn't want to worry her sister Lia—Frida's mother. Not just yet anyway, not until she knew something—anything she could tell her. It had taken enough joint cajoling between herself and her niece to convince Lia that her daughter was a big girl and that Bryndis could be responsible for her. Being the younger sister, Bryndis had always had to meet her older sibling's standards of how to be a grown up. Nervously, she looked at her phone again—still no messages.

It had been such a bizarre day. Staring at the four walls of the airport waiting room, with nothing to do but sit and worry, Bryndis started to replay it all in her mind. She followed the security agent's request and wrote down what she could remember about her day in the notepad—randomly at first—and, after a while, she began to feel a little better. The day's events were beginning to organize themselves in her head.

She wondered where Holt could be and what condition he was in. His place had certainly been thoroughly ransacked. However, there hadn't been any indication that she could see that any bodily harm or violence had occurred, at least not in Holt's apartment. She was glad she'd accepted Tony's final offer to stay and deal with the police in the morning while she'd gone back down to the bookshop. Betty Jo had left in a huff when she'd told her that Holt wasn't there. She'd scrawled a quick "Classes and gym closed this morning" note and posted it on the front door of Furst Fitness. Bryndis had planned to wipe her hands of any doings in Holt's life. *Let his brother Tony handle it,* she'd thought. She'd had enough of getting those two boys out of scrapes.

Still, something nagged at her. Tony had come rushing in, wanting the Munro book for his class that he'd said was due to start in half an hour. Then when they'd gone upstairs, he'd claimed to have the first hour of classes free. Odd. Was it a lie and, if so, for what reason? Bryndis made a note about that on another page of the notepad as she sat in the airport waiting room. She'd never thought to question Tony's motivation at the time; she was just grateful that he'd taken over waiting for the police, especially after the disturbing encounter with that Rambler fellow. Then there was the matter of Holt's cell phone. It wasn't like Holt to leave it behind. After they'd found it, she'd given it to Tony and wondered if he could crack the passwords on it, perhaps to discover clues to Holt's whereabouts. That phone went everywhere with Holt and he always kept it turned on. It had actually been a bone of contention in his and Bryndis's relationship.

She recalled when they'd come to the mutual decision to break up, she'd been ready. The relationship had become a constant bickering back and forth without mention of a committed future. It couldn't get much worse. She wanted to move on. Try as she might, however, to put her feelings about Holt aside, they had a history and their tiff the night before hadn't helped. His pride and bravado would often puff up and get in the way. He'd been so short with her when he couldn't find his key last night, she didn't even want to remind him of where he kept the spare one hidden in the wood trim. At the time, she'd decided to let it go and go back to her own place.

She'd been mulling these things over back at her shop, when she'd suddenly remembered spying the mystery box of chocolates that she'd tossed on the top of the burnt pastries in the waste basket. The box, still sealed up and glossy, had taunted her. No matter who'd sent them, they looked good, and they were an expensive European brand. She remembered looking around to see if there was anyone there to see her take them out of the trash. *Some times call for emergency chocolate*, she'd thought, *and this is one of those times*. She'd remembered double-checking the box and giving it a thorough wipe. However, when she opened the package, a strong, strange, almost eye-stinging odor overwhelmed her and she quickly closed up the box and tossed it back in the waste basket. *That's certainly not the way high quality chocolate is supposed to smell,* she'd said to herself.

Giving the offensive gift a push much further down into the pile of trash so that no one else would be tempted to sneak a nibble, she'd decided to line up her paperwork and plans for the Midwest Book Lovers' Conference—happy for the distraction. She'd turned on her laptop computer on the shelf behind the counter and pulled up her hotel confirmation emails, stopping only briefly to serve the coffee klatch crowd taking up her one large communal table at the back. The Book Biddies came in every Thursday morning, each ordering just one cup of coffee and nursing it through their hour-long book club meeting. At least they bought their books from her, so it wasn't a total loss. She'd then gone online and perused St. Louis restaurant and shopping sites, thinking of things to do with Frida outside of the conference proper. As usual, surfing the net proved to be a great mind filler. She'd made a reservation at a casual restaurant that looked like it would be fun for a teenage girl—hip, trendy, with so many five-star ratings that it looked like a BeDazzler had attacked it. *Even if the food was bad,* she thought, *it will give us something to talk about.*

She'd written all of this in the notepad she'd been given as she sat there all alone in the airport waiting room. She'd also added that Tony had brought the pair of police officers down to her shop when they were done looking over Holt's apartment. Tony's phone had rung as soon as the officers had started talking to her. She'd tried to listen to what Tony was saying— wondering, hoping it was Holt on the line. Tony had responded in short, curt answers, his face reddening as he spoke, eyeing the police, and then turning his back to continue the conversation. All she could make out were the words *he, missing,* and *fine, you do that.* One of the policemen seemed to notice Tony's phone behavior while the other one gave The Neglected Word a quick once over and asked Bryndis short questions, including one about the encounter with Rambler. She'd remembered then that she had the ripped piece of Rambler's tie-dyed shirt in her pocket and she pulled it out and gave it to them. They'd nodded, and she'd assumed her answers fit with Tony's answers because they didn't pursue the questioning for long. Then they'd asked her about her last encounter with Holt, pushing for details about their relationship. The Book Biddies stopped their conversation at this point to have a good listen to her answers, even though the officers had asked their questions quietly. Seemingly satisfied that she had nothing pertinent to add to Tony's story, but, she noticed, still eying Tony, the police said they'd keep a lookout for Holt but that his "messy apartment and car in its parking space weren't sufficient evidence to indicate foul play." Following this disclaimer, they'd left. Bryndis then questioned Tony about the phone call he'd received. He'd brushed it off, claiming it was nothing and then he'd left in a hurry, saying he had to get to the high school, forgetting all about the Alice Munro book that he'd wanted so badly earlier.

Bryndis returned to her computer, wanting to focus on her own life and on having fun with her niece. She scrolled through the Midwest Book Lovers' Convention website, perusing the directory of exhibitors—210 in all. She liked dealing with smaller and indie presses, and was pleased to see some of her favorite publishers listed. They always had the most interesting books and took risks with up and coming authors. Business had been good lately, and with a little money in the kitty, she planned to make several purchases for the shop—treating her customers and maybe herself to a couple of old classics. Frida, the Brontë fan that she was, would get a kick out of that. Bryndis's eyes zeroed in on one vendor—The Curiosity Shoppe—which was appealingly described as "an old-time book lovers' dream haunt" so she clicked over to the convention exhibitors' map site to locate it. It was Booth 153. Wait a minute. Wasn't that the number on the post-it note she'd found in that book titled *Expo* in Holt's apartment? Could it be the same one as the Midwest Book Lovers' Convention? She'd have to check that out.

Now, still alone in the airport office, she paused from her note writing to recall the rest of her morning. She'd gone to see Aunt Snædis at Modiste around noon, bringing her a bowl of mushroom barley—the soup of the day. That was about the only thing that had gone smoothly. They'd spoken about the plans for Snaedis to cover her shop during the conference and for that afternoon when she needed to pick up Frida at 3:00. She knew she was leaving her business in the right hands, and The Neglected Word would remain neglected in name only during her absence. The two women were close and discussed Holt's disappearance, with Bryndis filling her aunt in on the details of the morning—including the ransacked apartment and the mystery foul-smelling chocolates. Snaedis had been around for most of Bryndis and Holt's relationship history—the break-ups, make-ups and fights in-between. Snædis usually stayed neutral, listening without passing judgment as Bryndis blathered on, sounding out her own conclusions. Today, however, Snædis couldn't help but give her own opinion about what she'd lately seen of Holt.

"Bryn, dear," Snaedis had said cautiously, taking a deep breath, "I know it's not my place to interfere, but surely you've noted a change in Holt's behavior. He's been short and moody, not as easy going as he usually is."

"Auntie," sighed Bryndis, "you're preaching to the choir."

"Yes, dear, the angel choir you are indeed," she agreed, "but some of those friends of his—my lord! Not impressive, if I do say so myself. I remember seeing one gentleman who reminded me of a reject from a Cheech and Chong movie."

"Auntie!" exclaimed Bryndis. "How would you know anything about Cheech and Chong?"

"I watch *Dancing with the Stars*," snorted her elderly aunt, as she moved smartly around her dress shop, straightening items on racks. Bryndis guessed that if she brought a ruler into her aunt's shop, she would find each dress exactly the same distance from its neighbor. "He had that stringy hair and those tie-dyed outfits straight out of the sixties. Goodness, you don't suppose he and Holt were smoking those bong things upstairs, do you? I couldn't bear to think of my proper little shop being downwind of all that weird smoke."

Bryndis had smiled at her aunt and had assured her that her store's reputation was intact and then had left when she'd realized that she needed to get moving if she was going to pick up Frida at the airport on time. After she'd returned from Modiste, she gave the web a final quick search on her laptop. She saw no traffic or flight delays and figured this might be the one bright spot in her day. It was a 90-minute drive from Harpshead to the St. Louis airport, and Bryndis knew her way around the facility's parking garage, so she still had plenty of time. She puttered around the shop until about 1:00.

However, once she was on the highway she realized there must have been an accident since her last online road check. Not only that, but her well-loved Saab had been threatening to overheat in the stop-and-go traffic. It liked to go, letting the horsepower outrun the carbons. She knew it might be time to trade it in, but it was a gift from her parents when she'd started college. It was her old reliable, most times, but not today. She'd checked her phone that she'd tossed on the passenger seat—2:45 p.m.

"Hang in there, Swede!" Bryndis had coaxed her vehicle. The traffic kept moving erratically. The cars moved a few feet and then stopped again. All the idling had made the engine's temperature gauge rise, and it stayed dangerously high.

Then out of nowhere, the cars in front of her started going faster and she'd followed suit. The weird thing was that she hadn't come across any fender benders or vehicles in the ditch or on the side of the road to indicate the reason for all the halting traffic. Unfortunately, the unseen delays had made her arrival at the airport closer to 3:30 p.m. She'd rationalized at the time while hurrying from the parking garage to the terminal that maybe Frida's plane would be late. *Sometimes it takes time for them to land, taxi in,* she mused. She took a deep breath, and considered that with all that was involved in flying these days, security checks could hold up arrivals too. The reality, as it turned out, was that everything but her had been right on schedule.

Now, much later, she sat in the quiet waiting room feeling guilty and she sighed, exhausted, as she brought her head down on the desk. Suddenly, the door opened and a tall man in a pristine Missouri State Trooper uniform came in. "Ms. Bryndis Palmer?"

She licked her lips and tried to swallow, but with her mouth dry, all she could do was nod.

He introduced himself as Detective Sergeant Tomas Royland. "We have news."

Chapter Five
by B J. Gilbertson

Darkness surrounded Frida. Sounds of muffled activity echoed around her from a nameless void. Footsteps seemed to draw closer; from which direction, she could not tell. She withdrew further into herself, curling her knees up to her chest. A tear welled up in her eye and began to trek its way down her flushed cheek, but then was absorbed completely into the piece of cloth that had been tied around her head, around her ears and eyes. Frida was afraid. No, she was *terrified*. Why was this happening? What was going to happen to her? She desperately wanted her mother. Another tear began its lonely journey.

Two strong hands grabbed her firmly by the arms and pulled her up into a sitting position. She felt herself being propped up against a hard surface. She did not resist; she did not cry out. Her hands were tied behind her, and with her fingertips, she ascertained that she was sitting up against a wooden surface of some kind. Two voices began speaking back and forth, so low in volume, she couldn't make out what they were saying. She knew they were men's voices. Nothing more. She rested her back against the wooden surface and waited, her eyelashes brushing back and forth against the cloth around her eyes. She felt someone lift her blindfold up, slightly over her ear, and she began to tremble.

"Frida," a man's voice said. "If I remove this blindfold, do you promise to be a good little girl?"

She nodded her head.

"Say it." The voice was low and guttural.

"I promise," she said.

Her blindfold was lifted free, and despite the low lighting in the room, she had to close her eyes for a minute to allow them to adjust. Frida slowly looked around, keeping her eyes low. She was on a bed and sitting up against its headboard. It was a nice-sized bed, bigger than the one she slept on at home. She raised her eyes and found she was in a rather small, red room. Dark red. A depressing red. There were no windows and only one door. Directly opposite her was a table resting snugly against a wall. A tall, wooden standing lamp occupied the corner to the right of the table, and was the only source of light in the room. The lampshade was also dark red, so the amount of light in the room was relatively low. There were two wooden chairs—one of which was being occupied by a man, sitting just to her left, next to the bed. In his hand was her blindfold. Standing behind him by the door, was Elwin with his hands crossed.

The seated man leaned forward and smiled.

"Do you know who I am?"

He was an older man. Frida guessed in his fifties. He wore a long, dark grey overcoat. Like gangsters wear in the movies. He even had a fedora hat clasped in his free hand, resting on his knee. He had fine, white hair, slicked back with gel. His eyes were grey, his facial features were sharp, and his body lean and crooked. When he smiled at her, his eyes seemed to pierce her skin like a scalpel. She knew immediately that this was a man of consequence. However, she did not recognize him and shook her head nervously.

He smiled another wicked smile. "Say it."

"Oh, sorry…no."

"Good girl." He leaned back into the chair. "I find it's so much better when you actually speak while having a conversation, don't you?"

She was about to nod, but then caught herself. "Yes," she said.

"Good. Do you know why you're here?" His voice remained low, and she could hear an English accent, though it wasn't nearly as obvious or pronounced as Elwin's.

"No."

He watched her for a moment and then let out a breath. "No, I don't suppose you do. My name is of no importance, but you may call me Mr. Grey. Okay?"

Frida nodded and then quickly added, "Okay."

There was a soft knock at the door. Mr. Grey raised his hand which still held his hat and waved it once. Elwin took his cue and cracked open the door, stepping around to block any view. After checking to see who it was, he stepped back and opened the door wide. A man entered, pushing a metal cart into the room. On the cart was a tray of food, a glass of what looked like juice, and silverware. The man slowly wheeled it over to rest in front of the table. Elwin reached beyond the door and brought in Frida's bag, which she knew had previously been placed in the trunk of the limo, and set it down on the surface of the table. Elwin whispered to the cart-pushing man who nodded, and then left without a word. The door closed and Elwin resumed his position. Frida could smell the cooked food and her stomach began to ache.

"I took the liberty of searching through the items in your bag. I hope you don't mind?" said Mr. Grey.

"No. It's okay." Right now, all she wanted to do was go home.

"I knew you'd understand," he smiled. "I must say, you're not exactly what I expected. No iPod, no cell phone, no laptop, no Kindle, no earphones. You're not a typical teenager, are you?"

Frida bristled a little bit, but said nothing.

"You have an interesting choice of books too. *Jane Eyre*, Villette, and what was it? Ah, yes, *Wuthering Heights*. A Brontë fan—both Charlotte and her sister, Emily. Unusual reading material for a girl your age. One gets the sense that you must be a very special girl, Frida."

Frida had calmed down a little since the blindfold had been removed, but she refused to allow herself to become comfortable with this man. "Thank you," she said guardedly.

Mr. Grey leaned forward and tossed his hat on the foot of the bed. He clasped his hands before him and looked intently at the teenage girl.

"It is on the subject of books that I wish to speak to you," he started. "I love books. I love reading them, collecting them, selling them and sharing them. I love the smell of books. The feel of a hard-bound, leather book resting snugly inside my hand. I love everything about books."

Frida listened. *Where is this going? What does he want?* She tried not to show her fear.

"What is your favorite book, Frida?"

Frida hesitated. But she realized that it couldn't hurt to tell him that. "It's right over there…in my bag. *Jane Eyre*."

"So, it's not *Anne of Green Gables*, *Charlotte's Web* or *Nancy Drew*? Haven't you read these books?"

Frida raised her eyebrow. "Yes. When I was eight."

"When you were eight." Mr. Grey started to laugh. He turned to look at Elwin and laughed. "When she was eight." Elwin smiled and moved his body weight over to his other foot. "I love it," Mr. Grey continued, looking back at Frida. "When you were eight." He laughed a bit more and then sat back further into his chair. "So, Frida, why is *Jane Eyre* your favorite book? What does she mean to you?"

"She was strong, smart. She had to grow up in difficult circumstances," Frida answered. "She found fortitude inside of herself to continue, even when she didn't want to sometimes. She was ahead of her time. She survived grave illness. She learned what true love was and she married a man despite his own handicaps and weaknesses." Frida stopped and smiled. "She was my kind of woman."

Mr. Grey nodded approvingly. "Very good! It's refreshing to see someone your age with their priorities in the right place."

Frida looked at Mr. Grey. "What is your favorite book, Mr. Grey?"

Mr. Grey smiled, almost like a sneer, and leaned forward.

"I was hoping you'd ask," he said. "The Bible."

Frida frowned. *The Bible? Him?*

"I can see you don't believe me," Mr. Grey continued. He leaned back into his chair. "But it's true. In fact, I was hoping you might know where I could find a copy. I understand that your Aunt, Bryndis Palmer, owns a book store. Am I correct?"

Frida nodded.

"Say it."

Frida let out a deep breath that belied her calm demeanor. "Yes. That is correct. But I don't get it. All this just to get a copy of the Bible?"

"Oh, not just *any* copy, my dear. A very special, *rare* copy of the King James Version of the Bible. One that could change someone's life. Someone like me."

"How?"

Mr. Grey laughed softly. "I like you, Frida. I really do. You truly are a special breed. But, I don't like you *that* much. Let's just say I would never want for anything again with a book like that in my possession. The power it holds inside..." He trailed off.

"Why am I here? What are you going to do with me?" Frida was doubly afraid to hear the answers to these questions, but she had to know.

Mr. Grey looked at the frightened girl. "You could say you're our insurance policy. Do you know the man who was with you in the limo?"

"I think he's my aunt's boyfriend, Holt."

"*Was* your aunt's boyfriend. We thought he had this book. But he doesn't. Maybe it was on its way to him. Maybe your aunt has it." Mr. Grey narrowed his eyes. "Maybe *you* know where it is, or where it's going to be."

Frida cocked her head back. "Maybe I don't."

Mr. Grey laughed. "Maybe." He stood up and grabbed his hat and pulled his overcoat closed. "Maybe you should think about it. Really hard. I'll be back. Enjoy your dinner."

Mr. Grey turned and started towards the door. Elwin walked over and released the bonds from Frida's hands. She began to rub life back into her wrists.

"Find out where Shadow is and what he's found out," Mr. Grey instructed Elwin. "Tell him to report back ASAP. We may need him for a more....cosmetic assignment."

"You got it," Elwin replied. Mr. Grey walked out the door, followed by Elwin who locked it on his exit, leaving Frida alone and secure inside the room.

Trapped, Frida thought to herself. *Trapped inside a red room. Just like Jane Eyre*. The dinner could be poisoned. But that wouldn't make any sense. They needed her. For insurance, as Mr. Grey had put it. She swung her legs over the side of the bed and walked over to the metal cart and its contents. She lifted the lid to see a healthy serving of smoked turkey, mashed potatoes and corn...piping hot. There was even dessert. A slice of pumpkin pie. Almost like Thanksgiving. As she served herself a plateful, she thought back on the events that had led her to this point.

After Holt had been unceremoniously thrown into the back of the limo with her, she'd remained pressed up into the corner of the seat furthest away from him. She'd been scared out of her mind. When she'd been sure he didn't mean her any harm, she'd hidden her face and cried. She'd felt a hand touch her shoulder, and she'd pulled away.

"It's okay," he'd said. "It's all right. I'm not going to hurt you."

Frida remembered looking up, exposing only her tear-filled eyes. Holt was looking down at her with an expression of mixed emotions. He looked confused, yet compassionate, and obviously in pain. A nasty cut under his right eye was swollen into a big, purple bump on his cheekbone. He had blood on his shirt, which was torn at the shoulder.

"You're Frida. Lia's daughter, aren't you?"

Frida had nodded.

"I thought so. I don't understand. Why are you here?"

She'd shrugged and sniffled.

Holt had closed his eyes. "I'm so sorry you were dragged into this mess," he'd said. He'd opened his eyes. "Do you remember me? I'm a friend of your aunt's."

Frida had nodded. "I remember you."

Holt had half-smiled and touched her hand reassuringly. "Don't worry, Frida. I'm not going to hurt you. I'll do my best to get you out of this. I promise."

Frida had sat up and hugged Holt close. "I'm so scared," she'd whispered.

"I know. I am too."

Frida had sobbed on his shoulder while Holt had held her.

The car had stopped. Looking up, they saw Elwin walk to the door and open it, allowing sunshine to spill inside. The car was parked on what had appeared to be a remote road next to a field of weeds and grass.

"If you care for this girl as much as I think you do, then you'll do what I tell you," Elwin had said.

Holt had gritted his teeth in defiance, but nodded. "Do as he says, Frida. Don't be afraid."

Elwin had reached inside his pockets and procured strips of plastic and cloth. After they'd both been blindfolded and their hands tied behind their backs, Elwin had shut the door and they'd heard the car locks snap back into place. Within seconds, the limo was moving again. Frida had noticed the windows were so darkly tinted that anyone passing by could look straight at them and not even know they were inside. She knew that her aunt would have reported her missing by now, and that the police would be looking for her.

After what had seemed like an hour, the limo had come to a halt. She'd heard Elwin open the door. Frida had felt his hands around her arms, guiding her out of the limo. He'd closed and locked the door. "Walk," he'd said.

With shaking knees, she'd done as instructed and walked.

"Stop here," he'd said.

She'd stopped and waited. She'd felt for sure she was about to be killed. Her legs had grown weak and she'd nearly crumpled to the ground. But the blow never came. She'd heard something creak in front of her.

"In front of you is a portable sanitation unit. Do you know what I mean?"

Frida nodded.

"Go inside and use the bathroom. I don't know when you'll have access to a bathroom again. Understood?"

Frida nodded. He released the plastic band from around her wrists. She went inside and relieved herself. When she was done, Elwin put the plastic band back on her wrists and took her to the limo and repeated the process with Holt. Within minutes, they were both in the back of the limo, locked inside, reblindfolded, and moving again.

After what felt like another couple of hours, the limo had slowed down and was moving at a slower pace. The sounds of traffic around them had intensified. *We must be in a city*, she'd thought to herself. *But where?* Finally, the limo came to a stop. She could hear Elwin talking to another man. The door opened and gags were placed into their mouths.

"If *one* of you makes any attempt to run, I'll kill you both. Nod if you understand." Frida had nodded. "Move 'em out."

Hands pulled her out of the limo and she guessed Holt was being pulled out of the car also. Cool air washed over Frida's face and through her hair. She couldn't tell for sure, but it had felt like it was night and she could hear the sounds of normal city life. They'd been quickly escorted down a ramp into what could have only been a building. But what building? Where?

They'd been led down hallways, some longer than others. Sounds of clanging metal and steaming air could be heard through the walls, coming from some far-off room. Voices from people busy with their chores accompanied these sounds. It sounded to Frida like a large kitchen. Were they in a restaurant? A hotel maybe?

Frida had been taken into a room and dropped down onto what felt to her like a bed. The gag had been removed, but the blindfold and wrist band had remained. A door had closed behind her and all she'd heard was the sound of her heart pounding in her chest and her own breathing. She'd heard nothing else. Holt must have been taken to another place or room. She'd remained that way until Mr. Grey had come in.

Now, back in the present, she took another bite of her smoked turkey. Why did this Mr. Grey want a copy of the King James Version of the Bible, and what was so special about this particular one? Why did he think that Holt would have it? Why would she be insurance? None of this made sense to her.

One thing was sure. Her eventuality would be death. She'd seen Mr. Grey's face. She knew what Elwin looked like. No matter what, they wouldn't let her go alive. She was young, but she knew that much to be true. She had to find a way out. She needed to escape. The child inside of her caused her to slouch over and cry. Then, she made herself stop crying and she sat up, wiping the tears from her eyes. *Jane, I need you now. Help me.*

She sat there for a minute studying her surroundings. No windows. No telephones. There wasn't even a fire sprinkler or alarm system in this room. The only way in or out of the room was that door. How could she get out? Or get a message out for someone to help her? There had to be a way. She looked around until her eyes settled on her luggage bag on the table. Suddenly, her mother's words echoed in her head. "You'll appreciate it later." Frida smiled. *Thank you, Jane.*

Twenty minutes later, the man came back for the metal cart. He checked the tray and plate for notes or other hidden clues. Satisfied that there were none, he opened the door and left the room. He locked the door behind him and pushed the cart back down the long hallway towards the kitchen. But, Frida's bag was missing its pink and lime green bow. Because, unknown to him, it was tied snugly to a rail on the metal cart that he was pushing.

Chapter Six
by Helen Grochmal

To her surprise, Frida was getting sleepy, very sleepy. The thought crossed her mind that she'd been drugged—not enough to knock her out—just enough to lower her alertness.

In a little while, Elwin came in the door, tied her hands back up and put a gag in her mouth. He pulled her up from the bed. She staggered and leaned against him for support as her mind screamed at this indignity that her helpless body could not prevent.

"We're going to a book convention in a nice hotel, Frida Bonita, so I need you to be quiet like a lady while we move into a room there. You know the penalties for being a bad girl. Remember, we know where your aunt lives too." He picked up her bag to take it with them.

They made their way through several long hallways. On the way, Frida heard two people talking in a kitchen area through an open fire door that would normally have been closed.

"Look at the ribbon on this cart. Must be from some wedding we catered. What awful colors—pink and lime green!"

"Just throw it out."

Frida gasped silently as they passed unseen by the workers, out an exit door to an alley where she could see the limo waiting. Elwin made sure the door behind them closed. Dragging Frida's bag while he continued to hold her, made exiting awkward for him. He started to pull the bag and Frida down the exit ramp.

Before Elwin could stand her in front of him, in an effort to appear normal, Frida suddenly fell sideways against the railing of the exit ramp. Anyone looking at them would see Frida's youth and possibly notice that her hands were bound.

And some people did see. Two elderly women had just exited their car in the alley. They were walking toward the street when they saw Frida leaning over the railing with Elwin pulling on her from behind. At this point, the women were at the lower end of the ramp, directly behind Elwin.

"He's kidnapping that girl!" whispered the older woman to her friend. "Do something!"

The women hustled closer to the ramp and the older one stuck the substantial umbrella she was carrying between Elwin's legs.

Elwin toppled, falling backwards down the ramp, conveniently hitting his head on the corner of the base of a stone column. The women caught Frida as she fell backwards when Elwin released her, and they all landed in a gentle heap at the base of the ramp. All three heads turned and looked over at Elwin. He wasn't moving, and it certainly looked like his days of menacing anyone were over.

"Let's get out of here before anyone comes out to look for him," said the older one softly.

The two women took hold of a shaking Frida on each side and helped her upright as her hands were still bound. They made their way back to their car which was parked illegally a few feet beyond the limousine. The younger one got in the driver's side while the older one guided Frida into the back seat.

"Lock the doors, Madge. Then get us out of here," advised the older woman to her friend in the front.

Madge did as she was told, pulling the car around the limo, out of the alley, and into the street. They drove a few blocks, going through several busy intersections, as Madge appeared to be looking for a side road they could take to get them away from the alley and anyone who might be following them.

"What should I do, Bella? Find a police officer? Go to a hospital?" Madge asked, as she looked nervously back over her shoulder.

In the meantime, the older woman, Bella, had removed the gag from Frida's mouth.

"Do you need a hospital, dearie? Were you, uhm, hurt in *any* way?"

"No, no. I'm fine. I was kidnapped by a group of people who are looking for some kind of special Bible," Frida mumbled. "Are you helping me?"

"Goodness, yes," said Madge in her blunt voice from the front seat as she took another backwards glance at the cars behind them. "Can't you tell?"

"Yes, we're helping you, young woman," Bella cut in gently. Then she answered Madge's earlier question. "We can't just grab any policeman, Madge. Whoever's involved—this gang that kidnapped her—might see us with this young lady on these busy streets. We'd better be especially careful right now. We'd better find a police station or a hospital perhaps."

"I'm fine, really," said Frida. "I don't need a hospital. I just want to find my aunt. My aunt's probably looking for me. No one hurt me except for tying me up."

Madge almost hit a parked car in her nervousness. "I don't know where a police station is!" she shouted, and then began crying. "I don't know this town! Oh, Bella, I can't drive much longer in this horrible traffic."

"You know what, Madge? There were lots of motels we passed as we were driving into St. Louis. Why don't you just go back that way? We'll get a room in an out of the way place where we can talk about what to do and how to help this poor girl. But stop if you see a police station."

Madge took a deep breath, made a U-turn at the next light, and they headed back out onto the Interstate. They didn't find a police station, but Madge managed to find a small motel on an out of view side road off the Interstate.

"Don't park in front of the hotel. We don't know what anyone saw back there in that alley. There are cameras everywhere now," said Bella.

Madge parked in the small lot to the side of the motel.

"You both stay here. I'll check in," said Bella. She got out of the back seat, circled around to the front of the two-story motel and headed into the lobby. After ten minutes or so, Bella returned waving a room key. She climbed back in the car and Madge re-parked it almost exactly in front of their first floor room. They managed to sneak their new charge into their room without event.

Two chairs and two double beds were among the furnishings. Frida seemed wobbly, so the women sat her down on the bed. Bella and Madge moved the chairs over beside Frida. Bella hadn't managed to get the wrist restraints off of Frida yet.

"Would you get our bags from the car, Madge?" said Bella. "I have scissors in my toiletry bag. But, be careful out there."

Madge headed back to the car and Bella asked the girl her name.

"My name is Frida. I'd just gotten off an airplane on my way to visit my aunt. The man you knocked down that ramp kidnapped me at the airport. And he kidnapped Mr. Furst, my aunt's ex-boyfriend. I think he killed him." She started to sob. "Please call my aunt. She must be worried sick about me."

"We will, dearie. Let me get you some water first. Have you eaten recently?" Bella went to the small bathroom and removed the plastic cover from a drinking glass, filled it with water, and returned to Frida.

"Yes, they gave me turkey and pie, but I think it was drugged. I was very tired. I'm feeling better now though."

Madge came in with the bags and put the chain up on the door. She pulled out a small pair of scissors from a small bag and quickly cut Frida from her plastic hand ties. Then, the women waited silently as Frida drank the whole glass of water.

"I have a cell phone in my bag. Do you want to use it to call your aunt?" Madge asked.

"Wait, Madge!" said Bella. "Before she calls anyone, don't you think we should discuss what to tell her aunt when she calls her? We want to be sure to avoid those ruffians. They may be following us, maybe even her aunt too."

"Oh," said Frida, crestfallen, realizing she might still be in danger. "I hadn't thought about that. They did say they know who my aunt is and where she lives." She was starting to wonder who the old women were.

"I'm Bella Luchek and this is my neighbor, Madge Miller," announced the older woman, apparently reading Frida's mind. "We were going to a convention in St. Louis together to save money. We'd just parked in that alley to have lunch at a restaurant around the corner when that horrible man dragged you out. Now tell me, dearie. What is your whole name and your aunt's? Do you know the phone numbers we should call?"

Frida got a tablet with a pencil from an end table near the bed and began writing down the names and phone numbers—stopping every once in a while to massage her sore hands.

"I'm Frida Flynn from Santa Barbara. I was going to meet my aunt Bryndis Palmer who lives in Harpshead, Missouri. She was taking me to a book convention in St. Louis."

"The Midwest Book Lovers' Convention?" asked Madge.

"Yes," replied Frida, "I believe so."

"That's the same one we're going to," said Madge.

"Of course, it's the same one," added Bella. "How many book conventions do you think are held each weekend in St. Louis? But, go on, dear. We interrupted you."

"Anyway, before my aunt could pick me up at the airport, I was kidnapped by that man—his name is Elwin. Another man in that building where they were holding me was Elwin's boss, I think. He told me to call him Mr. Grey. He said he was looking for a King James Version of the Bible that my aunt's old boyfriend—Holt Furst—seems to be connected with. Mr. Furst was taken hostage with me too, and Mr. Grey implied that they had killed him. I think they were going to kill me too because I had seen their faces." Frida stopped and shivered noticeably.

"Shouldn't we report to the police that we bonked that Elwin fellow?" Madge asked Bella.

"Bonked? Bonked, Madge?"

"All right. K...killed," said Madge, visibly uncomfortable.

"Don't look so upset, dear. His demise—if he's truly dead—was merited from what we've heard about him so far," replied Bella, somewhat clinically. "I'm sure his confederates in that building will discover and dispose of his body soon enough, so I don't think we need concern ourselves with him again. His passing seems providential, don't you think? Besides, it was an accident. We certainly didn't intend for him to fall to his death; we merely were attempting to assist Frida here. And speaking of our young friend here, although I don't think she needs a hospital, a doctor's visit might be in order, don't you think, Madge? After we're sure she's safe, of course."

At that moment, Frida handed them her list of phone numbers.

Bella's next remark surprised them all as she perused the list. "Frida! You know, I believe I know your aunt. I think I met her at a book convention a while back. I remember that I admired her a great deal. Let's call her right away to let her know you're okay."

Frida said, "Please tell her about Mr. Furst."

"I will, although if she has a relationship with this Mr. Furst, who you say is involved in this mess, then she may be involved herself—albeit unwittingly. And that would complicate things," said Bella. "She might be under watch by the gang. We don't want her to be kidnapped too or for her to unknowingly bring the gang here to us. We need to be cautious in what we say."

"What should we do then?" Madge was clearly frustrated.

"Let's see," said Bella, biting her lip. "We have to get Frida to safety without the gangsters finding us. They will surely be on the lookout for her at train stations and airports and such. We must call her aunt to tell her she's safe, of course. I'd feel safer if Frida and her aunt were under police protection. However, if we notify the police about Frida's kidnapping, I'm afraid they'll just send her back home to Santa Barbara and then we'll never be able to find out anything. I'm thinking that maybe we can sleuth all this out better ourselves."

"Frida, something tells me that your Mr. Grey may be looking for this strange King James Version of the Bible at the Midwest Book Lovers' Convention too. Don't you think?" said Bella. "Why else would he and his gang be here in St. Louis this weekend? We may be able to find information in and around the convention that will offer us some clues as to where that Bible is and or who Mr. Grey is—and what has happened to Mr. Furst. One thing I'm certain of is that you won't be truly safe until we know the whole story and Mr. Grey and his gang are caught. My guess is a good first place to start is at the book convention."

"Bella, we can't do this all ourselves," said Madge.

"My Aunt Bryn will help!" cried Frida. "She has a room reserved for the two of us at the convention and she loves mysteries."

"She *may* be able to help us," Bella agreed happily. "An 81-year-old woman and a 67-year-old woman and a teenage girl are not going to be able to fight gangsters with physical force. We have to *think*! Clues are our métier, not martial arts with thugs."

"I'm hungry. We never did get our meal. I can't think until I eat," complained Madge.

"Okay," replied Bella, grumbling. "I'll go get something from the convenience store next to this place. I don't think we should eat in a restaurant; Frida might be recognized. I'll be back with drinks and sandwiches. Then we can make our calls. Don't open the door until you hear my voice."

"I should go, Bella. I'm younger," volunteered the taller Madge.

"But I walk better than you do since I got my two knees replaced. You've done enough with the driving. Don't worry, Frida. We'll figure out a plan as soon as we eat. Let's talk about other things for a while." Bella appeared to want to calm Frida down for what might lie ahead.

While Bella was gone, Frida mentioned that she'd lost her books in the confrontation with Elwin.

"So you like to read, dearie?" Madge asked. "What do you like?"

"Well, *Jane Eyre* is my model. I always ask myself, 'What would Jane do?'"

"Oh, yes, Brontë," said Madge. "I myself prefer Jane Austen. I read everything I can about her. I used to like Charlotte Brontë until I read what she'd said about Jane Austen. I'll never forgive her for criticizing Austen."

"What did Charlotte Brontë say about Jane Austen?" asked Frida, fascinated.

"She said things like, 'The passions are perfectly unknown to her.' Of course, that wasn't as bad as what Mark Twain said about her, though, and I still like to read him."

"What did he say?"

"He said, 'It seems a great pity that they allowed her to die a natural death.'"

"Oh." Frida pouted.

They heard a knock on the door.

"It's me. I'm alone. Let me in," called Bella.

Madge removed the chain. Bella bustled in with the sandwiches and drinks. They all sat with bags of food in front of them.

"I got us all hot tea," noted Bella. "It's so comforting."

"Some Irish whiskey in it wouldn't hurt," remarked Madge.

Bella gave her a look of reproof. "What were you talking about while I was gone?"

"Jane Austen and Charlotte Brontë. I convinced Frida here of the superiority of Jane. Didn't I, luv?"

Frida was about to protest when Bella intervened.

"There is no competition," said the older and possibly wiser Bella. "We can appreciate the merits of both. One is classical, the other romantic; it's like comparing Mozart to Beethoven."

The tea and food eventually did their work. Everyone relaxed; Frida perked up.

"So let's clean up and make our calls," said Bella. "I don't think we can wait to hear what the local news on the television says. We have to act now."

After a few minutes, they were organized. They sat in a circle, Madge with pencil and paper. Luckily Madge's cell phone had a speaker.

Bella dialed Bryndis's number. She answered immediately.

"Bryn Palmer speaking."

"Hello, Ms. Palmer. This is Bella Luchek. You may not remember me but we met at a book fair once. I have good news for you. We've rescued your niece who was kidnapped."

"Oh, my God! Is she all right?" exclaimed Bryndis over the phone's loudspeaker.

Frida laughed. "Hi, Aunt Bryn! I'm fine."

"Oh, Frida! Are you okay? I was so worried!"

"Yes! Thanks to Ms. Luchek and Ms. Miller!"

"Frida, may I talk to you alone, please?" asked a worried Bryn.

"Of course," said Bella, handing Frida the phone and pulling Madge towards the bathroom to give their young charge some privacy.

Once alone, Frida reassured her aunt that she was indeed safe, then gestured for the two friends to return, handing Bella back her cell phone. Bella explained to Bryndis what had happened and their present situation.

After a pause for Bryndis to take all of it in, Bella continued, "The reason we didn't call the police is that we're running away from the gang that kidnapped Frida and we're not sure what to do and we wanted to talk to you about it. It was such an unsettling experience. We first wanted to be sure Frida was safe. We fear we may have been followed and we're also worried that the airports and bus stations or even you might be under gang surveillance. We needed to plan what to do. We were afraid that if we contacted the police, they might send Frida back right into danger. So, we decided to eat first and call you so you can call Frida's family if you think it's safe to do so. We believe we're safe here now, but we don't know how we should proceed. I assume you reported Frida's disappearance to the police?"

"Yes, of course," replied Bryndis. "When she didn't appear at the airport, I notified airport security and they contacted the local police. Her disappearance has been reported but. . .I haven't called her mother yet."

"Is your phone being monitored by the police now?"

"No, not my cell phone."

"Think about the danger we all face," cautioned Bella. "You may need to be watched by the police or go somewhere safe where this gang can't find you. The same for Frida. Oh, I don't know! Maybe you should just put Frida on a plane back to California—"

"No!" yelled Frida. "I don't want to go back home! I'm part of this and I deserve to be a part of its solution."

Bella said, "Oh, and, Ms. Palmer, I'm so sorry to tell you this. The worst news of all is about your friend, Holt Furst. I told you about how he was kidnapped along with Frida. When Frida was being held in the building, Mr. Grey talked to Frida about Mr. Furst in the past tense."

While Bryndis was silently processing these horrifying developments, Bella quickly began discussing their plan. "We were hoping you could come join us if you can get here without anyone following you. We have some ideas about this Bible that this Mr. Grey is looking for. We assume the book convention Elwin was taking Frida to is the Midwest Book Lovers' Convention—"

"Yes," agreed Bryndis over the speaker, "I can't imagine there are any other book conventions going on in St. Louis this weekend. I have a room reserved for Frida and myself at the convention hotel."

"That's what we thought. Madge and I are registered there too. So we can all do some investigating at the convention hotel," continued Bella. "We can co-ordinate our investigation from our room or yours—or somewhere else. We don't think any of the gang saw us when we knocked Elwin out, so Madge and I should be safe out in the open. You have to decide, Ms. Palmer. You can call the police, if you want. But Madge and I might have some trouble with the police if you do. We did knock out—or possibly even kill—one of the kidnappers."

There was a short pause. Bryndis was obviously contemplating her options. Finally, she spoke.

"I'm sure you're right and we might be able to get to the bottom of this mystery at the convention. And I even think I have a clue we can start with. I found a strange note in one of Holt's books. It said something about an 'Expo Bth 153'." I checked the convention website and Exposition Booth 153 belongs to an Old Curiosity Shoppe. So, that would be the first place I'd check. I have some other ideas too. But I'm very confused right now. Frida's safety is the most important to me and then looking for Holt—I just can't accept that he's dead. There should be a way to involve the police to protect Frida, but still allow us to investigate on our own—after all, right now, the police are using a lot of manpower searching for Frida. It's not right keeping the fact that she's safe from them. Of course, they still need to investigate the kidnapping—and find out what happened to Holt. Let me think. Let me think." She sighed and the three women in the hotel room could sense her fear and concern in the silence that followed.

"The police will take it all out of our hands if you call them, I'm sure. The gang may have some contacts within the police force too," cautioned Bella.

"Auntie Bryn," begged Frida, "please let me stay with Miss Luchek and Miss Miller tonight and you can join us here tomorrow and we can all go to the convention together. Please, please!"

Listening to her niece, Bryndis suddenly made up her mind. "All right! I'll be there tomorrow, Frida. You can count on me. Now let me talk to Miss Luchek."

Bella gave Bryndis the name and address of their motel. "If you decide the police should be informed, please let us know, and make sure it will be police who can really protect us. I can't wait to get Frida safely into your hands. It's a miracle we got her away."

"You may be right, Bella," said Bryndis. "It may be best for all of us if we wait a day or two before we tell the police so we can at least check out the convention. At the very least, I need to get my niece actually with me so I can tell her mother she's okay firsthand. Let me make some calls. Will you all be okay for tonight?"

"Yes, of course," they all responded.

"Okay, I'll be there tomorrow," said Bryndis with finality. They said farewell and hung up.

The women got ready for bed but stayed dressed in their day clothes in case anything happened during the night. Bella decided to play guard and sat on a chair but eventually fell asleep with her head on a table.

In the morning, they checked the news on television. There was nothing mentioned about the death (or injury) of Elwin (or anyone who might have been Elwin). The women assumed this meant that either he hadn't died or that his body had been disposed of by the gang shortly after the women had snatched Frida from the alley.

There was also no mention of Frida's kidnapping. "I wonder why the news isn't broadcasting Frida's kidnapping," wondered Bella.

"They may not be able to officially declare it a kidnapping yet," suggested Madge. "Isn't there that rule about the person has to be missing 48 hours or something before the police get involved?"

"But her aunt reported her disappearance to the authorities," said Bella.

"It's probably just a matter of time before it's all over the place," said Madge. "Oh, my! We'll have to disguise Frida. When we take her outside, we'll have to be certain that she isn't recognized. How about we act like we're just two old ladies with our niece?" The three of them headed out the door and quickly got into their car with Frida in the backseat, and headed in the direction of the nearest fast food establishment.

"That will be hard," noted Bella with a scowl. "Playing two old ladies, I mean."

Frida reminded the two women that Jane Eyre had taken flight from Mr. Rochester. She told them again of her admiration for Jane Eyre, and the fact that she felt different from most girls her age. "I like Elizabeth Bennet too, of course, and Emma," she added to prevent one of Ms. Miller's friendly rants but was unsuccessful.

"You bet, Frida. Now you're talking. In Jane Austen's day, women couldn't get jobs except as servants and governesses—and sometimes the only way they could survive was to inherit money. I don't think Jane Eyre ever smiled." Madge went on to describe how she'd been disappointed in love a lot when she was younger. Frida was spellbound listening to the old lady ramble on about her life and her love of reading.

"Jane Austen seems very *nice*," said Frida eventually. "I like her but I still like Jane Eyre the best."

They all laughed as they stopped at a hamburger joint to eat breakfast in the car.

"Now about getting you that disguise, Frida," suggested Madge. The discussion of how to do that and what the disguise should look like took up the drive back to the motel.

The morning passed. It was decided they needed to get a wig for Frida and some clothes and toiletries. Madge went out to get some things from a local thrift shop—including, believe it or not—a short brown curly-haired wig.

By the time she'd tried everything on, Frida was now convinced that Jane Austen was way *nicer* than she'd originally thought.

"Did I tell you I burned my bra back in the good old days when feminists were real feminists?" Madge exclaimed.

Before Bella could change the topic, a knock came on the door.

"It's me—Bryndis! It's okay to open the door."

The next minute, a curly-wigged Frida was in Bryndis's arms as the door was re-bolted behind them.

Chapter Seven
by Tim Hall

The convention hotel was beautiful and grand, particularly the exhibition hall.

"Why are we here again?" asked Frida who looked a bit like Orphan Annie in her curly-haired get-up.

"Because it's the only clue we've got right now, Frida," replied Bryndis.

Bryndis saw the anxious look on her niece's face. She motioned around the convention center, then smiled tolerantly at Frida in an attempt to reassure her.

"Don't worry, dear. What can they do in a big building like this, filled with people?"

"Uh, Aunt Bryn? They kidnapped me from an *airport*."

Bryndis's smile dropped. "They did, didn't they?"

"That's right," Madge chuckled. "Lucky we snatched you back. And we left that big creep lying in an alley."

"But what if there are more of them this time, or they have guns?" asked Frida.

"Remember what they say," Bella interjected. "'The best defense is a good offense'."

"Sometimes the best defense is not looking for trouble in the first place," scowled Frida.

"Frida, honey," Bryndis assured her, "I know you're scared. I'm scared too. But Bella is right. And this time, you have back-up. Remember, there's safety in numbers! And as long as they think we're mixed up in all of this, we're really never going to be safe. We've got to find out what these criminals—whoever they are—want. And all we know is that it's some kind of Bible, and possibly connected with this Booth 153. And that Holt is somehow mixed up with it too."

"Besides, we still don't know if we killed that Elwin creep or not," Bella added. "If he's dead, I say we go straight on to Mexico. I'm too old to go to the clink."

"Oh, I don't know," Madge said thoughtfully, "I always thought those prison stripes were rather slimming."

"It depends on whether they're horizontal or vertical stripes," Frida countered sincerely.

Bryndis consulted the map for The Midwest Book Lovers' Convention that came with the giveaway tote bags each of them got when they entered. "Let's see. If this is the entrance, here, then I think we have to go two rows over and then about halfway down. Are you going to be okay, Frida?"

Frida nodded and smiled. "I'm okay." She pulled down on her wig which was sitting a bit crooked on her head.

As the women started in the direction Bryndis had suggested, Bella sighed. "I hope I find something good to read here," she said. "At least, something better than the last book I read. It was terrible."

"What book was that?" Bryndis asked, always curious as to what a potential customer might feel about a particular book. Bella ignored her and looked away. As they continued to walk, Madge came alongside Bryndis.

"She doesn't like to talk about it," she whispered.

"About what?"

"The last book Bella read was *Fifty Shades of Grey*."

"I didn't know what it was about," Bella protested weakly. "I thought it was a hair-coloring guide."

"Oh, that's nothing to be ashamed of," Bryndis said and shrugged. "Anyone could have made that mistake."

"Yes," Madge added, "but then she learned there are more books in the series, and she doesn't know how to order the others from her bookstore without dying of embarrassment. Turns out our Bella really enjoys a good *hair dying* saga!" She snickered.

"I can never set foot back in *that* bookstore again," Bella said sadly. "They must already think I'm a pervert. What if someone I know saw me buying another book in that series?"

"That would just clinch the pervert story, wouldn't it?" Madge nudged her friend.

"Stop it, Madge!" scowled Bella, looking shamefully at the ground.

"I'll put copies in a brown paper bag for you at my shop," Bryndis whispered to Bella conspiratorially.

Bella loved intrigue. "Would you really?"

"Of course." She winked at Bella and the older woman beamed with satisfaction.

The women turned down an aisle, moving at a cautious pace, keeping watch for any suspicious characters.

"Just act casual," Bryndis advised. "I think we're coming up to the booth on the left."

"Which one?"

"It's supposed to be right here." Bryndis checked the map again. "Isn't it? Maybe I'm confused."

"No, you're right, Aunt Bryn. Look." Frida held up a small sign that was lying on the table in front of the empty booth. "There's a printout right here. Booth 153. The Curiosity Shoppe."

"Except nobody's here."

"Wel-wel-welcome!" sing-songed a voice. The women jumped. A tall man at the next booth grinned at them. He was wearing a garish checkerboard suit and a bright yellow hat.

"I hope you ladies didn't come all the way here just to look at an empty booth. I assure you, my books are far more interesting."

"You got any Bibles?" Madge asked loudly. Bryndis tried to discreetly shush her. The man in the yellow hat frowned.

"No, alas, I do not. I'm afraid that if you're looking for religious materials then I cannot help you."

"We're not looking for religious materials, wise guy," Madge snapped. "I said we're looking for a Bible."

"I see. And why are you shopping for Bibles?" he demanded.

"Why are you asking?" Madge's eyes narrowed to suspicious squints. "You trying to get funny with us?"

"Heavens, no."

Bryndis tugged her gently by the arm, but Madge wouldn't budge. "Come along."

Bella walked up to the man's table and picked up a book. "What do you sell, mister?"

The man beamed at her. He produced a card and handed it to her. Bella held it close to her nose. "Mighty…Fine…Artists," she read slowly. "Books by the educated, for the wise." She looked up. "What's that even mean?"

"It means," the man demurred patiently, "that I only carry books written by authors with MFA degrees or higher."

"What's M-F-A?"

"Master of Fine Arts. It's simply *de rigeur* these days if you want to be somebody in this business. I also specialize in fake memoirs."

"Day-rig-what?" Bella asked.

"Essential, my dear. I simply cannot abide texts written by semi-literate barbarians."

"So no Bibles?"

"I should say not."

Madge was studying the yellow-hatted man intensely, as if the three letters he'd uttered were some kind of clue. "What's this MFA thingy have to do with writing well?"

"Everything, madam."

"Did Jane Austen have an MFA?"

"Oh no, of course not."

"Charlotte Brontë?"

"Dear lord, no."

"How about Ernest Hemingway?"

"Nope."

"Agatha Christie?"

"Good heavens, no."

"Then what good is it? Sounds like a bunch of hooey to me," she said with finality.

Bella cupped her mouth and projected a loud whisper at the man. "Do you have any of those *Fifty Shades of Grey* books?"

The strange man ignored Bella. He strained at the collar, barely keeping his composure, as he addressed Madge.

"Hooey? I'll tell you what's hooey, madam. It's having any nincompoop with an Internet connection being able to publish whatever drivel spills off their fingertips while they're hung over from swilling cans of cheap beer. Self-publishing and print-on-demand are killing whatever remains of a genuine literary culture in our society! That is the real *hooey* clogging the pipes of cultural progress, my dear. I am attempting to clear those pipes, nothing more. I'm a literary plumber, if you will."

"Yeah, well I think I'd like to flush you," hissed Madge.

"Please leave," said the man.

"That reminds me. I gotta find a john," said Bella. "Mister, where's the john?"

"Does J. K. Rowling have an MFA?" asked Madge.

"Most definitely not. And as for the bathroom, I have no idea. Now good-bye; I need to attend to the non-crazy people here."

"Who you calling crazy?" asked Madge.

"Millions of Oprah viewers, apparently," he sighed.

"My aunt here has a bookstore," Frida interrupted, trying to keep the conversation going. "And she has lots of great books."

"Oh?" The man glanced at Bryndis with mild disdain. "A fellow tradesman? How interesting."

"She has lots of nonfiction books too, about real stuff that happened. But I like fiction."

"You don't say."

"I'm sorry to bother you like this," Bryndis said, "but are you sure you don't know anything about The Curiosity Shoppe? It was supposed to be in the booth next to yours. Nobody has been here all day?"

"I didn't say that," the man sniffed. "In fact, there were several men here asking about that booth just before you arrived."

Bryn felt her blood run cold. "Men? How many?"

"Two or three. Maybe more. Rather ugly fellows. Rough looking, if you get my meaning. Definitely not in the market for any Bibles, that's for sure."

"That's what you think," Madge said.

"Thanks for your help," Bryndis added quickly. "Come on, Frida, ladies, let's not bother the nice man any more."

The man picked up a business card from his table. "Take one of my cards, in case you want to come back and insult me some more." He smiled kindly at Frida. "Not you, of course. You're sweet." Frida took the card. *Mighty Fine Authors, based in Iowa.*

"Thank you," she said. "If I'm ever in Iowa, I'll be sure to stop by."

"Just be sure to come *alone*," the man smiled, and waved them away.

"That was a bust," Bryndis said. She didn't realize until then how much her heart was pounding.

"What a wacko," Madge laughed.

"You were very unkind," Bella said. "You might have tried buttering him up a bit; he might have given us some information."

"He didn't know anything." Madge sniffed. "Nobody with an MFA ever wrote anything worth a damn."

"You didn't even know what it was!" Bella laughed.

"That doesn't matter. Who the hell wants to read a fake memoir?"

Frida checked the convention map. "Looks like the bathrooms are downstairs. Aunt Bryndis, I'm scared. From what that man said, it looks like those men are here."

"Let's just stick together. We'll be all right."

The group found an elevator that took them downstairs. There were some panels going on there and some more exhibit tables. The four stayed together and went into the bathroom together, then rode the elevator back up.

"What now?"

"I'm hungry," Frida said. "Can we get any food here?"

"I think I saw a food area in the corner. Let's see what they've got," said Bella.

The ladies found the café area. There was a small selection, but enough for each of them to get something. Madge and Bella staked out a table with a view of Booth 153, and a minute later, Bryndis and Frida carried trays over and set them down. Pizza, pretzels, coffee, iced tea, and Diet Coke. Frida had just started eating a slice of pizza when Madge peered into the distance.

"Is that one of those men, come back to snoop around the booth?"

The others looked up. Frida gasped with fright. "I think that's one of them! Oh, Aunt Bryn, I'm scared!"

Bryndis was already pushing her seat back. "So am I, sweetheart. Come on, let's get out of here."

"And go where?" asked Madge. "The entrance is on the other side of the floor. We have no idea how many of them there are. They could have the whole place covered by now!"

Bryndis saw the emergency exit doors, next to the café which led to a small courtyard where a couple of people paced and sat, poked their phones and smoked.

"Come on, out here."

"Seems a shame to leave all this food behind," Bella said disapprovingly.

"We have no time. Come on!"

Bryndis led the others in a semi-crouched formation out to the patio area. Scattered about were a few large planters and small shrubs and trees, in a vague attempt at some kind of landscaping.

"We can't hide out here. Now we're trapped!" Frida was beginning to panic. Bryndis scanned the patio area and saw steps leading down from the rear. She didn't know where they went or if they would lead them to a dead end, but it might provide enough cover. It was the only chance they had.

"There!" Bryndis commanded.

The ladies almost tripped over each other scuttling over to the railing and making their way down the shady steps. To Bryndis's relief, the stairs exited to another opening; luckily they weren't sealed off. The four women got to the bottom and kept going. There was a small covered area that opened up to a desolate parking lot and the rear of the building that housed the loading docks for the convention center.

Madge peered around the corner of the building.

"I don't think they saw us," she said after a minute. "I think we lost them."

"Even so, we can't stay here for long."

Frida sat on the edge of one of the loading docks, swinging her legs. "What now?" She looked at her aunt expectantly. Bryndis thought for a moment, then took Madge and Bella by the hand.

"You two have been so wonderful, I can't even begin to tell you both how grateful I am. But I can't ask you to stay and endanger yourselves. I owe you both a tremendous debt, which I plan on repaying once we've settled this."

"What's she saying?" Bella asked.

"She's saying it's time for us to go," replied Madge.

"It's safer if we split up," said Bryndis. "We took two cars here, which was smart. But now we'll all be safer on our own. The bad guys have no idea who you two are, your names or any of the rest of it. I'm sure you'll be safe."

"Well, if you think it's all right."

"I know it is."

Bryndis and Frida hugged the two older ladies, and waved them off. Bella and Madge walked carefully back across the asphalt to the small staircase up to the patio.

"That was cool of you, Aunt Bryndis. Letting them go and keeping them safe."

"Well, however this mess started, it had something to do with Holt and nothing to do with them. I'm sure we'll see them again someday. Besides, you and I can move a lot quicker without them."

Frida hopped down from the loading dock. "Speaking of which, can we get out of here? It's still creeping me out."

"Of course."

They turned the corner and froze in their tracks. There, from across the asphalt, a van was driving toward them, fast. The man behind the wheel was not smiling. Neither was his passenger. Or the third man sitting between them.

Chapter Eight
by Joyce Oroz

Time slowed to a crawl for Bryndis as the grey van careened off the main street and squealed sharply around the drive-up circle in front of the convention center where she and Frida were glued to the curb. Bryndis grabbed the back of Frida's shirt, and yanked her back onto the lawn. They rolled backward six feet into a pile at the base of a tall tree. In that same moment, the van hit the curb and rolled onto the passenger side, wheels spinning as it scraped along the asphalt for several yards.

Bryndis lifted her head and watched the driver poke his ugly mug out the window like a scared rabbit.

Frida untangled herself from her aunt. "Oh my God! That's Elwin! He's alive! I guess Bella won't be going to jail after all."

"Was he the limo driver?" Bryndis asked, strapping her purse over one shoulder.

Frida nodded, and crawled behind the tree.

Bryndis pulled a pen from her purse and quickly scribbled the van's license number on her left wrist. "Let's get out of here while those guys are still shook up." She helped her niece to her feet and pulled her to a full gallop. As they ran, Holt's face popped into her mind—the sweet, thoughtful Holt she used to know.

The two of them skittered through the closest entrance door into the convention center. After working their way through the crowds of book-lovers and lookie-loos, they fell into a pair of soft chairs, part of an oasis of furniture for weary shoppers and convention-goers at the far side of the lobby next to the restrooms.

"Aunt Bryn, you look like you've been crying."

"Yes, I guess so," she blinked.

"It was scary, but why are you—?"

"Frida, honey, I don't understand it myself. I suddenly thought of Holt. We had quite a history together. I guess I need to feel sad for a while." A tear slipped over her cheek and down to her chin. She wiped it away. "Now, Frida, tell me who else you saw in that van besides that Elwin."

"I'm pretty sure I saw Mr. Grey. I recognized his hat," Frida said, still breathing hard.

Bryndis sucked up some air, and waited for her heartbeat to reset. "Did you recognize the guy in the middle?" Her words were barely audible.

"Well, I'm not sure, but the man in the middle looked like Mr. Furst—Holt. Of course, I only saw him for a little bit when we were tied up together in the limo. But I don't know why he'd be sitting up there in front with those two. I'm sorry if that makes you cry, Auntie."

"I thought I was imagining things." Bryndis let a few 'happy tears' flow. "But, I thought it looked like him too. So maybe Holt *is* alive. I wonder if he's a captive—or a gang member." Her gut feeling was that Holt would never be involved in something as sinister as kidnapping Frida. She wished she'd been more patient with him in the past. His intentions were usually good. She remembered times when Holt had helped her in the kitchen, and even waited on customers if she was too busy making soup or pastries. He'd brought her flowers one Easter, a shell bracelet from his trip to Hawaii and an antique box from his diving trip to Cancun.

"Aunt Bryn, you have a weird look on your face."

Bryndis smiled. "I'm thinking back to when Holt

brought me a present from Cancun a couple months ago. He told me that a Mexican fellow had pushed this very old-looking wooden box into his hands and asked for a few pesos so he could buy food for his family. Holt figured it was a knock-off antique but he felt sorry for the man and gave him a fifty-dollar bill. Besides, there was something inside the box."

"Why are you smiling, Auntie Bryn?"

"Because . . . I think I know what these jerks are after and . . . I think I know where it is. But first, I need to make a phone call. Do me a favor and just sit here quietly and read your book while I make a call."

"But, but...."

"Frida, please do as I say."

Frida dutifully remained where she was while Bryndis walked over by the elevators and placed a call on her cell phone. Frida tried to read her lips, paying no attention to the free book she'd picked up at one of the convention booths.

Bryndis dialed and Aunt Snaedis answered on the second ring.

"Bryndis, dear, I was just thinking about you. That silly young man, Weston Blake, has been asking about you—"

"Never mind that, Aunt Snaedis. I need your help right away. Go up to my apartment—you know how to find the key. There's a white Macy's bag stashed in my clothes closet way in the far back corner. I want you to take the wooden box out of the bag, put it into a large plastic container—you'll find a big green one under the kitchen sink. Dump the cleaning products out, put the box inside, seal it up and put the whole thing in the vegetable bin in my refrigerator. Got that?"

"Oh dear, the lead broke on my pencil. Okay, now I have a pen. Closet...bag...green container...vegetable bin—got it."

"That's not all. I need you to call a locksmith—Martin, not Ramsey. Ask Mr. Martin to install a dead-bolt on my front door ASAP."

"Yes, dear, Martin...dead-bolt...A...S...what?"

"Quickly, Auntie. Thanks. Love you." Bryndis hung up the phone and looked around to see if anyone was listening. Frida had fallen asleep with the book in her lap. There were so many things Bryndis wanted to do to try to track down Holt, but she realized that Frida needed to sleep and there was no way she would leave her niece for even a moment.

Bryndis's phone rang, startling her into the moment. It was Lia asking about Frida.

"Hi, Sis. Frida's asleep next to me, a book in her lap."

"Sounds like she's acclimating just fine. I'm already missing her. Her brothers drive me crazy, but I'm constantly thinking about my little Frida." Lia sounded calm and oblivious to the dire situation her daughter and sister were in. Bryndis saw no reason to alarm her. She planned to deliver Frida to her mother safe and sound in the near future. The sisters chatted a few minutes and then hung up.

Muffled sounds of sirens from a fleet of police cars and possibly an ambulance made Bryndis smile. She pictured in her mind the authorities questioning Elwin about his erratic driving. But that brought to mind the third man she'd seen in the van. Had she and Frida mistaken the man for Holt? Was it really her ex-boyfriend that she'd seen in the front seat, straddling the gearshift? Did he survive the crash?

Frida opened her eyes, yawned and closed the book. The ten minute nap would have to do. "What now, Auntie?"

"Let's go back upstairs to the exhibition hall and check on Booth 153 again."

There was no one there when they got to the booth. But Mr. Checkered Suit and Yellow Hat was in his booth grinning like a Cheshire cat wearing ugly clothes.

"Ladies, nice to see you again. Are you looking for those ding-a-ling women you were with?"

"Ah, not really...do you know where they are?" Bryndis asked.

"Right over there—Booth 174, next aisle over," he pointed.

"Thanks. Did anyone show up to work in Booth 153?"

The man shook his head. "But I can find a nice book for you." He pointed to some colorful covers in his booth.

"I thought you only carried the classics," Bryndis said, turning to include Frida in the conversation. But Frida wasn't there! Panic surged as she whirled around, scanning the long lines of booths.

"I only carry *good* books," he corrected her.

But Bryndis didn't hear him because she was already two aisles away, desperately searching for her niece. As she came closer to Booth 174, she saw Frida hugging Bella. The ladies welcomed Bryndis and there were more hugs all around. When the old ladies asked how things were going, Bryndis told them about the close call at the curb, and Frida led them to a bank of floor-to-ceiling windows for a view of the main street below.

Four police cars with red lights flashing were scattered about the circle drive. A tow truck waited patiently at the curb for the officers to finish investigating the van which had already been righted onto all four wheels. There were no crash victims in sight, no one in cuffs, and no one in the back seat of a cruiser.

"Looks like the scoundrels got away," Madge said.

Bryndis saw the obvious and struggled to keep her

panic under control.

Frida looked at her aunt's pale face and knew there might be more trouble. She put an arm around Bryndis, expressing her solidarity in finding answers to so many questions.

When the four ladies arrived back at Booth 153, the old salesman in the neighboring booth scoffed and rolled his eyes like a checkered whirligig. If he was flirting with Bella, it was a pitiful display. However, Bella recognized it as flirting and began her own version of the game.

Bryndis gave Madge her business card and asked her to call if anything new developed. She and Frida then said their goodbyes again, explaining that they needed to get back to Harpshead as quickly as possible. Bryndis bit her tongue, thinking maybe she should not have mentioned where they were going.

Anxious to leave the convention center, Bryndis and Frida hurried across the second floor, making their way to a hallway that led to the parking garage. In the dimly lit garage, the old Saab never looked so good. Bryndis fired up the engine, zoomed out of the parking garage, picked up Highway 70 heading south and left St. Louis at a good clip. She wanted to avoid the Interstate which she assumed would be the first place the gang would look for her once they realized she and Frida had left the convention. She watched the sunset, as silhouettes of the occasional barn and farm house replaced the big city lights. Stars sprinkled the sky. Harpshead was only a few hours away.

* * * * *

"Frida Bonita, I'm afraid we have a problem."

"What? I mean, I guess I fell asleep, Auntie."

"We had over half a tank of gas when we left the

convention center. The needle went to empty in less than fifteen minutes. Something's wrong. Dang! The motor's cutting out. I'll drive it as far as I can."

"Auntie Bryn, there are headlights following us...."

"I know, honey; I saw them. There's an exit coming up for Vandalia. See the lights ahead? When I say so, be ready to run," Bryndis said as she white-knuckled the wheel with a quick right turn.

The Saab sputtered half-way down the exit ramp and then rolled, quiet as a cotton ball, into the gas station at the corner. One last drop of gasoline dripped onto the pavement.

Bryndis set the brake, grabbed her purse and flew out of the car, accidentally bumping into Frida as they rounded the building. Unfortunately it was a help-yourself kind of gas station, and the office was dark.

"Now what?" Frida choked, her eyes wide, straining to see in the dark.

"It's going to be okay. We'll cross the street to that Laundromat. Looks like the whole town closes at dusk here, all two blocks of it." She grabbed Frida's hand and pulled her toward the street.

The headlights paused at the bottom of the exit ramp. The dark sedan started up, crossed the street and pulled in at the curb in front of the Laundromat.

Hearts pounding, Bryndis and Frida ran across the dark empty street into the steamy, well-lit Laundromat. Bryndis pulled Frida through the building to the back door.

"Locked!" she yelled.

They turned to their right and entered a grubby little restroom and closed the door. Not daring to turn on a light, Bryn flipped the lock and leaned her full weight against the door, bracing her feet against the base of the toilet.

Frida's teeth chattered uncontrollably.

"Hang on, sweetie," Bryndis whispered in the dark. She heard the front door open and close, footsteps and voices. She shivered.

"Auntie, I hear women," Frida whispered.

Bryndis put her ear to the door. It was true; the voices sounded female. She listened again and thought she recognized one of the voices. She carefully unlatched the door, opened it a crack and peeked out.

"Oh, my! Frida. It's okay, honey. Come on out."

Frida couldn't believe her tearing eyes. She was close to fainting with relief. Instantly she and Bella were in a bear hug.

Madge wrapped an arm around Bryndis and asked why she was shaking.

They all sat down in white plastic chairs and ate junk food from a vending machine. Bryndis explained that she wanted to get herself and Frida out of the convention and home quickly, before the gang figured out where they were going. Then their car had died and here they were. They'd thought that Madge and Bella were the gang and were following them. Madge then offered them a ride. Bella offered to drive, but suggested that maybe Bryndis should drive because she was younger and she and Madge had terrible night vision. Everyone agreed that Bryndis should drive.

"I've always wanted to go to Harpshead," Bella said. "I like small quiet towns."

"I'm just happy to be out of St. Louis," Madge added.

"And we're so glad you found us," Frida said, cocking her head to one side. "How did you find us?"

Madge laughed. "Remember the guy wearing yellow? Well, the three of us were talking after you left—flirting in Bella's case. Anyway, this man—a very disheveled man, I must add—was looking around The Curiosity Shoppe's booth and when he found no one there, he ran up to Mr. Yellow Hat, said a few words to him, handed him a note and ran off. Mr. Yellow Hat shared it with us because he remembered us being with you."

Bella grinned. "I think he likes me."

"Never mind that, Bella; the note might be important. We tried to find you to give it to you, Bryndis, but when we reached the parking garage, we watched you speed down the ramp and turn right at the street. We jumped in our old Ford here. Bella slammed her bunions on the gas pedal and here we are."

"Your broken tail light was a big help after the sun went down," Bella said. "It was exciting, especially since I normally don't drive at night."

"I owe half my grey hair to you and your driving …." mumbled Madge.

"Now, Madge, settle down," reproached Bella. "If it weren't for my driving, we'd be stuck in a couple of rocking chairs on the front porch right now."

"Ladies, do you have the note?" Bryndis cut in.

"Sorry, dear." Madge fumbled around in her over-sized purse, pulled out a small piece of wrinkled paper and handed it to Bryndis.

Scrawled on the paper were the words: *Bryndis, meet me at my place. Holt.*

Bryndis flushed as half a dozen different emotions collided inside her brain. Was this note really from Holt? Had he escaped the kidnappers? Or was this just a ploy on the part of the kidnappers to get her? If it was from Holt, he must be running for his life, and he wanted to see her at his apartment. Had he seen her when the van had crashed? And if so, why would he leave her a note with this old vendor? There was only one thing to do. Luckily, Bella had already offered her their old Ford, making it possible for them to head straight to Harpshead.

The old ladies settled into the backseat with Frida in the front. They'd be in Harpshead in no time with Bryndis driving over the speed limit.

Madge stretched her neck to see the dashboard. "We're traveling very fast, aren't we, dear?"

"Now, Madge, let the girl drive. We're so old we don't know what speed is anymore. Besides, we don't have that much longer to live anyway…."

"I get the hint; it's just that there are headlights right on our tail," Bryndis said.

"And a twirly red one too," Bella added, as Bryndis brought the car to a stop at the side of the road.

The officer took his time getting to her window. "Miss, did you know this is a sixty-mile-an-hour zone?" he said as he examined her driver's license.

"Actually, I forgot to look at the speedometer. This isn't my car and I'm not used to—"

"Miss, keep your speed down, okay?"

"Okay," Bryn squeaked, a smile spreading across her face.

The officer went back to his patrol car. Bryndis continued her drive home. An hour later, Madge commented on more lights behind them. Bryndis wondered again who was behind the headlights.

Chapter Nine
by Joe and Pam Reese

Nine thirty. A half hour since they'd left St. Louis, heading south on State Highway 61 to Harpshead. Bryndis knew she could have taken Interstate 55, but— no, not with this car. Besides, the highway they were on seemed somehow safer, somehow more secretive. And so the towns flowed past, one by one: Herculaneum. Festus (yes, there really was such a town). Bloomsdale.

St. Mary's. Ware.

The road was two-lane and blacktop, bordered on each side by impenetrable walls of yellow pine, and punctuated at five to ten mile intervals by the above-named communities, each of which consisted of house trailers, small houses, larger houses, the village mansion, the downtown, the village mansion on the north side, large houses, the McDonalds, the Wal-Mart, small houses, house trailers, and once again the forest.

And so she drove on.

The headlights behind them did not vary their distance, and Bryndis somehow forced herself to forget about them. She could not outrun them; that was certain. And as for driving ever more slowly—well, she tried that once, fifty, then forty-five—

They kept their distance.

The others in the car slept.

And so there was only she and her mind—that plus the two tunnels boring ahead of her into the black Missouri night by the car's unchanging headlights.

It did no good to think of Holt, of course, because all that was past.

But then, there was always Mr. Faulkner with his sad eyes and whiskey-laden philosophy: "The past is never dead. It isn't even past."

And it wasn't.

So there was Holt up in the front seat with her, not as he was these days, of course, curt and dismissive and incomprehensible and devilishly attractive and devilishly devilish...

...but as he was when they'd met as sophomores in high school.

The kisses in the vacant lot behind the First Presbyterian Church, acacias all in bloom, the senior class having performed the town's fiftieth Mayfete, and both of them having served as Duke and Duchess of the tenth grade.

God, how long ago was that?

And how good it had all been.

And how completely it had all changed.

"Aunt Bryndis?"

For an instant Frida replaced the ghost of Holt as, curled like a cat in the front seat, she asked, "How long now?"

Bryn checked the odometer and shook her head. "We're close now. Just a mile or so more."

"Are those headlights still back there?"

"Some headlights are back there. Could be anybody."

Frida said nothing, but she darkened the entire car. Bryn did not understand immediately why. It was more than those cave-like penetrating eyes and her crow-ebony hair. No, it was her way of looking out over the glowing dashboard and into the world, which, vacillating between various kinds of evil potentials, as it always seemed to do for a fourteen-year-old, had chosen the one it was going to take.

Kidnap.

Possible murder.

Okay, so be it, Frida seemed to be saying. *Bring it on.*

Silence again in the front seat, semi-snoring in the back from Madge and Bella, whose ribs seemed to have become cemented to the armrests.

And so what should she think about now? More of Holt? No, something lighter.

Crime and evil.

Why would two men—perhaps three or four—kidnap a young girl, and possibly murder a man who, except for Bryn's emotional life, had never done anyone a bit of harm?

For a Bible?

Well, what were the possibilities concerning that?

Why would such people want a Bible—a particularly old one at that?

One thought came immediately to mind: spiritual growth and renewal!

The Bible was such a wonderful book! The psalms, the story of Joseph, Jesus and the parables—why, the whole secret of life lay in its pages. Perhaps Elwin and Mr. Grey, as well as the enigmatic Rambler (if truly, the tie-dyed man had anything at all to do with this), were seeing a way to return to Christ, and, unable to procure a Bible in a normal bookstore, had decided to turn to kidnapping and homicide in order to get one.

Or no, perhaps that was not it after all. Since 'that' was patently absurd. But what then? Why would they want a Bible? God only knew.

Excuse, Bryndis told herself, *the pun.*

But she did not do so.

* * * * *

In a little under five miles, they passed the sign:

HARPSHEAD
THE MOST BEAUTIFUL LITTLE TOWN ON
THE MISSISSIPPI!

How often had Bryndis seen that sign, native Harpsheadian as she was? And how often had she speculated that, absurd as it was, it was probably true? She loved her home town.

They crested the hill, and...and there before them lay the Mississippi River. The sight of it overwhelmed her the way it always did, always would.

"Wow," she found herself whispering. A childlike thing to say.

But then, elemental things always drew her back into childhood.

There it was, almost as wide as the sea itself, placid and winding, a barge floating far to the north, another one disappearing around a bend to the south, the moon's rays glittering on water that seemed, from this distance, absolutely motionless.

The narrow road descended, a little steeper now, a turn here and there—down to a pier, toward which could be seen chugging a night ferry boat with no cars on it.

"We could," she said, sliding the car into the narrow slip that said, 'Autos board ferry here, "have crossed over the river on the new bridge. I thought it might be better to go over on the ferry."

"Why?" asked Frida.

"Anybody who wants to follow us will have to come right onto the ferry with us. At least, we'll see who we're dealing with. And if they don't want to take that chance, then they'll just have to wait until the next ferry. We'll be long gone. No way they can follow us."

"That's smart, Auntie."

Yes it is, she told herself, quite congratulatory. *Yes it is.*

"How do you figure those things out?"

"I read a lot of mysteries."

"Ever read one like what's happening to us?"

She shook her head. "No one would believe it."

The car reached the river's edge where the ferry's mooring had been set up. It stopped, motor still running, while the ferry chugged toward it and cut its engines, drifting along toward the shore.

There were no headlights behind them now. Nor were there any to be seen as they drove onto the ferry, or during the crossing, or as they drove up the far river bank and then rounded back onto the bridge and over it and back into downtown Harpshead.

They reached the west end of Broad Avenue. And now Main Street, festooned with banners, as it always was. The shops: Expressions by Claire, Clay Creatures, The Stink Shoppe, and then a left turn, taking them into the neighborhood where Bryndis's parents had lived all those many years ago.

It was not the richest part of town. No, the trees were not as stately and magnificent and the people were not as stately and magnificent. But both sets of living creatures—trees and people—had done all right for themselves. They were upper middle-class trees and people, who exuded in comfort and conviviality what they might have lacked in lineage and wardrobe. They shaded each other. Low to the ground, hardworking, and efficient, they shared a flora/fauna appreciation for cracked-with-time sidewalks, ambulatory and not decorative. The trees shaded these sidewalks not because they were obligated by God to do so, but because the sidewalks seemed to attract them down, invite them as it were. And the people walking on the sidewalks shared something in common with the trees themselves, not passing helter-skelter over the concrete on their way to some encounter or another, but standing rooted in it, as the sun set, and they chatted aimlessly about the turning of the earth.

It had been her neighborhood growing up, and she felt a curious certainty that she would be drawn back to it before her death.

Which, she found herself thinking rather sardonically, *I hope will not be soon.*

"Okay, everybody," she said, much as a parent to her brood, "we're home!"

And they were. The car turned from Avenue F to Congress and crawled to a halt in the white gravel lot behind her apartment above the bookstore.

"Already?" screeched one of the voices from the back seat.

"Well!" screeched the other. "You made wonderful time!"

"Thank you!" Bryndis answered. Was she screeching too?

And within five minutes, they'd clambered out of the car as well as octo- and sextogenarian legs could clamber, made it up the rickety-end stairwells, checked to be sure that no one had broken into the door lock— no one had—and gone inside.

It was a small apartment but it embraced and comforted them. Bryndis took a moment to contemplate and marvel at Madge and Bella, as those two fantastic creatures made their way around the living room, analyzing it as they would a long-forgotten tomb.

Madge, at 67 she had learned, was the younger of the two. She was in a way less memorable, but only in the sense that the Lesser Antilles are less memorable than The Greater Ones. But as it was, Madge was pretty unforgettable in her own right. She was quite tall, perhaps five feet eleven. But that was nothing, for that was possible. Impossible was her attire. She had on a baggy sweater which, with its vertical red stripes and horizontal white gashes and stars, looked less like a garment and more like a vast tent that some sultan had disassembled and was carrying over-the-shoulder.

And then there was her face.

That face, Bryndis mused, was as deeply and exquisitely wrinkled as a Kandinsky painting or a Stravinsky symphony, or, for that matter, any work of art whose creator's name ended in "insky."

This then was the woman who, folding her gangly and ungainly form around an overmatched armchair, sighed and said to her friend, "I wish I had a cigarette."

Upon hearing which, Bella gave a start. But the surprise in Bella's features was impossible to imagine without a grasp of the impossibility of Bella herself.

She could not, Bryndis estimated, have been more than four feet tall; and she looked like she was peeking outward and upward at the world from beneath an invisible fence.

And her smile…

The smile was perhaps more memorable than either stature or angularity. It was unchanging, unwavering, explosively, radioactively white. It took up half of her face, and exerted so much upward pressure that the eyes above it remained permanently squinted, small dark slits of mascara which ran down and away from her angular, slender nose, at another forty-five degrees.

She kept her gaze fixed upward and crookedly on Madge, an amazing feat for a woman with no visible eyes. She was a red and black-clad woman, and ageless. There was too much makeup (also red and black) to perceive her skin, and too much brightness to examine her character or demeanor. She could have been the governor's wife or a carnival ride.

"But Madge," she erupted, "you don't smoke!"

To which Madge merely sighed, saying, "I know. I never have. And I've always regretted that."

"But why do you want to smoke now?"

"I don't know. It would seem so dramatic."

"Still, if you've never done it before…"

"Well, dear, we must remember that you, to the best of my knowledge, have never stuck your umbrella between a man's legs, causing him to fall down a ramp and hit his head on the base of a stone column. *Before*, that is. And it did seem quite satisfying."

"Well. To me. Not to him."

"Still…"

The conversation wilted a bit. Finally, Bella said, "Isn't it strange that those two despicable men should have had such lovely English accents?"

Madge nodded. "I was thinking the same thing. Such accents bespeak courtesy and civility."

And for a time, the four of them simply breathed heavily, unpacked, talked about the impossibility of their all staying the night in this one apartment, talked about the impossibility of their doing anything else, and discussed the advisability of their calling the police. Which was certainly the thing to do.

Holt was missing. A gaggle of kidnappers was on the loose, very possibly, if one thought about it, in Harpshead.

And so Bryndis should probably have picked up the phone in her apartment, called the town constable who ten years previously had been the town's leading fullback and never gotten over it (having suffered concurrent swellings of the head and weakening of the intellect)—and said, "Hi, this is Bryndis, I'm over here at The Neglected Word—you know, next door to the

Laundromat. I'm the one who used to be shacked up with Holt except we aren't any more and I was supposed to pick up my niece Frida and take her up to St. Louis for the book convention but she got kidnapped and, oh, I forgot to tell you, Holt may be kidnapped too and somehow Holt got thrown into the same car as the people who kidnapped Frida because they wanted a Bible.

"But it's okay now because an eighty-year-old woman and a sixty-year-old woman beat them all up and we're all here in my apartment now not really knowing what to do. Can you help?"

Yes, that was what she could do. Actually, she had not the slightest idea of what she *should* do. So she was pretty much agreeable to almost anything when—with Madge and Bella having been given a bit of tea and with the apartment quiet—Frida came closer to her as they cleaned together in the kitchen and asked, almost whispering, "Aunt Bryn?"

"Yes, dear."

"I want you to remind me of something."

"All right."

"That line you're always quoting from Jane Austen. From *Emma*."

"Which line?"

"You know, when Emma is just standing there, looking out at the street in Highbury. Not seeing much. Or at least not realizing what she's seeing. And not seeing."

Bryndis smiled. "Yes. It's one of my favorite lines. 'A mind lively and at ease can do with seeing nothing. And can see nothing that does not answer'."

"And it means..."

"The truth is all around us sometimes and we don't see it. We miss the little things. And what we take to be the truth is a complete sham."

Frida nodded. "Yes. Yes. It's true. And, for the last few minutes or so, I've just been telling myself those lines. And saying, 'Think, Frida. Something's wrong. Something that doesn't fit. Something that you're not seeing.'"

Bryndis looked at her. "And?"

"It just came to me, Aunt Bryn."

"What did, darling?"

"When Madge and Bella were talking about Mr. Grey and Elwin? About their English accents?"

"Yes?"

"I never told them that those two men had English accents. And they never heard either one of them speak. So...how could they know about the accents unless they already knew Mr. Grey and Elwin?"

The two women—older and younger—stood, looking at each other.

Chapter Ten
by Julie Seedorf

Bryndis was about to respond to Frida's comment when a loud pounding broke the atmosphere. Bella let out a shriek from the other room, spilling her tea on Madge as she jumped up from her chair. Madge jumped up at the same time and, ignoring her tea-soaked attire, grabbed Madge and put a hand over her mouth. Bryndis and Frida entered the room, eyeing the door suspiciously.

Bryndis crept over to the door and placed her eye at the peephole. When she saw who it was, she opened the door. "What do you want?" she asked Weston Blake, as his hand was paused in midair ready to knock again.

"I've been waiting for you," he said.

"Why? And how did you know I was here?"

"I saw you come in with these women. But that's neither here nor there. Let us in," he answered as he started to push through the door.

Bryndis started to protest as he muscled his way into the apartment. Madge picked up a lamp ready to go to Bryndis's aid when a second figure followed Weston inside. All four women gasped. They were looking into the face of Holt Furst.

Bryndis ran up and embraced Holt, relieved that he was alive. "Holt, we thought you were dead! Look at you, all bruised and beaten. How did you get away?" Bryndis turned to Weston, "And how did he end up with you?"

Before Weston could answer, Holt looked up and saw Madge, still holding the lamp, and Bella. He turned, pulled out a gun, and aimed it at the two elderly women. Weston, Bryndis and Frida gasped and jumped back in shock.

"Holt, what are you doing?" Bryndis questioned. "Put that gun down; these ladies rescued Frida and helped us get back here!"

"Those ladies," Holt answered, "are with the kidnappers. One of them is even married to one. Call the police."

"No, no, you don't understand," Bella implored.

"Call the police, Bryn," Holt ordered.

"I'll call," Weston volunteered. "Holt filled me in while he was hiding at my house last night." Weston walked out the door onto the landing to place the call.

"I told you," Frida whispered to Bryndis.

"You're making a big mistake and putting your life in danger," Madge said to Bryndis. "We can explain."

Holt continued to hold Madge and Bella at gunpoint for a good five minutes without a word. All of a sudden, the quiet was broken as Weston re-entered, followed by a tall, big-boned man, sporting a badge on his shirt. This man was followed by two Harpshead policemen.

"Detective Morris Krill." The tall man offered his hand to Bryndis and then to Holt. "I understand these women are involved in your kidnapping?"

"Yes, they are, and they're the cause of all of these bruises," said Holt.

Bella and Madge gasped as Holt unbuttoned his shirt to reveal more bruises in addition to the ones on his face. "And they should be charged with attempted murder. I was grazed slightly by a bullet as I was attempting to get away from them." Holt held out his ankle and lifted his jeans to show the mark.

Detective Krill turned to the policemen and motioned toward Madge and Bella. "Take them downtown. I'll be there shortly to question them."

Bella cried out, "What he's saying isn't true! Don't believe him. Why would you lie, Holt—if that's who you really are?"

Holt laughed as they were being taken out the door. "And who else would I be?"

"I'll need all of you to come down to the station. I'll expect you there shortly," Krill advised them as he walked out the door. "You too, Blake. I want to know how you got involved in this."

Weston walked over to Bryndis and winked at her before asking, "Did you ever find out where the box of chocolates came from? Later, babe." Giving her another wink, he followed the detective out the door.

As they left, Tony Furst was attempting to enter, pushing the exiting group out of his way so he could get to Holt. Once inside, he ran up to Holt and grabbed him tightly. "You're safe! They told me you were dead, but you're safe!"

Holt grabbed Tony's arms and stepped back. "I'm back, baby brother. Did you think you'd seen the last of me?"

"We didn't know what to think when you didn't show up to open your business and then we found your apartment trashed," said Bryndis.

Holt ignored Tony and Bryndis and turned to Frida. "Sorry you got involved in this, uh. . . kid."

Frida eyed Holt suspiciously and nodded before turning to her aunt. "Can I talk to you, Aunt Bryn—privately?" she whispered.

"Can it wait?" said Bryndis. "You heard the detective. We need to go down to the police station. You were right to be suspicious of Bella and Madge. Your instincts are very good, Frida Bonita."

Before Frida could answer, Holt broke into the conversation. "Tony, could you take Frida down to the police station? Bryndis and I will meet you down there."

"But I really need to talk to you, Aunt Bryn," Frida pleaded.

"Just a minute," Bryndis said to the two men, "let me calm her down a bit." She took Frida into the kitchen.

"Something doesn't feel right," said Frida in a whisper. "Maybe I was wrong about Bella and Madge. I don't think I should leave you alone with Holt."

"Go with Tony and see what's happening at the police station. Just stay alert. I'll be fine with Holt. We'll follow you right away. I promise." She gave Frida a kiss on the cheek and led her to the door and watched as Frida and Tony left for the station.

Bryndis was about to follow them out the open door when Holt grabbed her arm. "Bryndis, I need to talk to you now that we're alone. You have to help me. My life depends on it and we can't tell the police. I'm sure those old ladies won't talk."

Bryndis unhooked her arm from Holt's hand and turned to look at him. "What's going on, Holt?"

"Where's that box I gave you with the Bible in it? I need to hand it over to those men or they're going to kill me."

"Then we should give it to the police. They can protect you."

Holt looked at Bryndis, thoughtfully furrowing his brow. After a long pause, he spoke. "You're right. Where is it?" he asked anxiously.

Bryndis led Holt into the kitchen. "I had it hidden when I heard that the kidnappers were after it."

"Where? Where is it? Um...the police will want it right away."

"Patience, it's right here in the drawer of the refrigerator." Bryndis opened the vegetable bin. She lifted out the container that she'd told Aunt Snaedis to hide. As Holt bent over to grab the container, his shirt rode up and Bryndis saw a small tattoo on his back at the waistband of his jeans. "When did you get that tattoo? You didn't have it before."

As Bryndis asked the question, Holt lifted the lid off the container. At the same time that Holt discovered the container was empty, Ceiko, Holt's cat, wandered into Bryndis's apartment through the open door. The cat gave a loud hiss, flexed her claws and attacked Holt's back like a mad lion. Holt jumped around to get the cat off of him, causing the empty container to fly through the air. As the container hit the floor, and Bryndis was trying to help get Ceiko off of Holt's back, Bryndis's cell phone belted out the song, "Itsy, Bitsy, Teeny-Weeny Yellow Polka Dot Bikini,"—the ringtone she'd designated for Aunt Snaedis.

Chapter Eleven
by Emma Pivato

Bryndis looked towards her cell phone just as Holt managed to grab the cat which he threw across the room. Bryndis picked up her phone and told Aunt Snaedis to hang on for a minute. Then she rushed towards the cat, but Holt grabbed her elbow.

"Forget the cat and don't answer that phone!"

Confused, Bryndis shoved the phone in her pocket to free her hands and asked, "What's wrong with you, Holt? What's driving you to act this way?"

"Just get me that Bible!" he spat.

"I don't know where it is since it isn't where I thought it was—but you're welcome to look for it," Bryndis said and moved towards the door, scooping up the cat on her way.

"You're not going anywhere," he said coldly, grabbing her by the wrists. "Who else has a key to this apartment?"

"*You* do—or your Doppelganger does," Bryndis whispered. She was really frightened now and she absolutely did not intend to tell him about her conversation and plan with Aunt Snaedis about hiding the box with the Bible in the refrigerator. Her aunt was old and her heart was not that good anymore. Getting caught up in this kind of a situation could be the end of the woman.

Bryndis waited anxiously to see how he would respond next. Maybe he really was Holt, she thought, and he'd had some sort of mental breakdown. Maybe the tattoo on his back was one of those temporary transfer tattoos and that was why the skin around it was not red. But then she remembered what Frida had said about Holt's nose when they'd been riding in the limo together when they were kidnapped. This 'Holt' had been beaten up, but not as badly as Frida had described—and his nose was definitely not broken. And why didn't he recognize Frida if they'd been together in the limo after they were both kidnapped? If somehow he was still really *her* Holt, then he'd know about Aunt Snaedis too—that she had a key to Bryndis's apartment. Finally, he responded.

"You *must* have given your door key to somebody else. Maybe a neighbor. What about the person next door? That would be the obvious one." He grabbed her by the shoulder and shoved her roughly out of the apartment, marching her to the apartment next door— Aunt Snaedis's. "Now, knock nicely on the door and announce who you are so we can get in there! Do as I say or I'll put a bullet right through that pretty little head of yours!"

Bryndis did as she was told, her heart thudding so loudly that she could barely raise her hand to knock. Her voice came out in a quaver and 'Holt' kicked her viciously. "No funny stuff."

Bryndis knocked again and called out, "Hello, Mrs. Sharpe. It's Bryndis." She had no choice but to use her aunt's last name as it was displayed prominently beside the door in a neat little name plate. But Bryndis would never address Aunt Snaedis so formally in real life. She only hoped her aunt would get the clue and not open up. There was no answer. Bryndis breathed a sigh of relief but she could see how agitated 'Holt' was.

"I *have* to get that Bible!" he groaned and then threw his weight against the door to force it open. Nobody was in the living room and he headed towards the bedroom. Bryndis's quick eye had noted that the deadbolt to her aunt's patio door leading to the fire escape was unlocked. As soon as 'Holt' was out of sight, she moved quickly and locked it, backing away from it just as quickly. Her aunt must have heard her outside her door with 'Holt' and gone out that way. Aunt Snaedis would never have left her patio door unlocked under other circumstances. She was very security conscious. Bryndis just hoped she was all right. She could hear 'Holt' rooting around through her aunt's drawers and her closet. She heard him moving the mattress and throwing things on the floor. She stealthily moved towards the door to try to escape. But he must have realized what she was up to and he came out of the bedroom, waving the gun, and grabbed her.

"Oh, no, you don't! If they find me, I'll give them you and tell them *you* know where the Bible is. Then maybe I'll have a chance!"

After a few more minutes of desperate searching, he said, "It's not here. Your store! I bet that's where you hid it!"

"No, Holt! Don't do this down there. You know how much that store means to me!"

"If you don't want me destroying your precious little store, just tell me where the Bible is. Otherwise, that's exactly what I'm going to do!"

Bryndis looked into his flat, dead eyes and finally she knew for certain. The tattoo could have been a temporary one. With all the swelling in his bruised face, Frida could have been mistaken about the nose. But never, never could her Holt have looked at her that way. Not after their fifteen years of shared memories—first love, first sex, supporting each other through setbacks and celebrating their successes together. Yes, their relationship had been up and down and was off now as lovers. But, even now, he could *not* not care. Bryndis laughed bitterly. In this case, a double negative really *did* make a positive.

But wait. Maybe this was a case of Dissociative Identity Disorder. Maybe this person in front of her was Holt's alter ego? Maybe that was why he'd been acting so strange lately? Even as she thought it, Bryndis knew it was not true. Holt could not have hidden a second identity from her all these years. Was the real Holt really dead? She turned to 'Holt' and asked, "What have you done with him? What have you done with the real Holt?"

But just then, they heard sirens and, seconds later, brakes squealing in front of the apartment. 'Holt' looked frantically at her, seemingly gauging his chances. Then he turned, unlocked the patio door, and rushed out and down the fire escape. Bryndis bolted out the front door and down the stairs to warn the police who were pounding their way up. They followed her direction and turned and raced down after 'Holt,' but by the time they got out to the alley, 'Holt' was gone. They began a house to house search but could not find him.

Bryndis pulled her phone out of her pocket to call her aunt, but realized the connection was already open. Aunt Snaedis must have pushed the button when it rang previously and before 'Holt' stopped her. Maybe her aunt had heard what was going on and called the police. Then she heard her aunt's voice shouting frantically, "Bryn, Bryn, are you okay? Is he gone?"

Bryndis collapsed against the wall of the stairwell, shaking violently. Her aunt appeared from the far end of the building. "What did you do with the Bible, Aunt Snaedis?"

"I watch those CSI shows," her aunt said, panting a bit. "I was pretty sure a determined crook would know to look through the fridge, so I hid it somewhere else— where he'd never find it!"

Chapter Twelve
by Steve Shrott

"Follow me."

Bryndis walked behind her aunt as she headed back towards The Neglected Word.

"You hid the book in my store? But that's the first place they'd look."

"You'll see."

Bryndis's forehead crinkled. She knew Snaedis to be a smart cookie, but how could she think that this would be a good idea?

Snaedis opened the door to the backroom of The Neglected Word, and marched inside, passing the tables with the boxes of books. Bryndis stayed close behind, but kept looking over her shoulder to make sure no one was coming after them. Each time she heard one of the old floor boards creak, she jumped.

As they reached the far wall of the room, Bryndis wondered where the heck this secret place was. Finally, her aunt stopped. "Here it is."

Bryndis looked around. "Where?"

Snaedis reached into her purse and removed a small knife. She stuck it into the wooden floor and ran it back and forth in an old section of plywood.

"What are you...?"

Her aunt lifted up a section of wood, revealing a tangle of ropes attached to its underside. "Look down."

Bryndis stared into the hole in the floor and gasped. "A secret room? How could I not know about this in my own shop? How did you know?"

"I stumbled on it when you were away; I didn't get a chance to tell you about it. Someone came around looking for a book—*The Grapes of Wrath*. I knew you didn't have it out front, so I came back here. When I was searching, my shoe got stuck in the wood on the floor. When I tried to get it out, I discovered the door. Just to let you know, I did find a copy of *The Grapes of Wrath* back here in the store room, but when I handed it to the guy, I saw that it was actually *The Apes of Wrath*—a book of short stories about monkeys. The guy took it anyway—thought it would be more fun than reading about the Depression in the thirties."

"Auntie, what could be in this underground room?"

"Come." Snaedis pulled a small flashlight out of her pocket and flashed the beam into the cellar.

"How?"

"This rope is actually a ladder." Bryndis looked at it and saw that there were rungs. Snaedis began climbing down, flashlight tucked under her arm.

"Auntie, should you be climbing down ropes at your age?"

"No problem, dearie. I was a gymnast when I was a child. I bet I could still do a triple somersault flip." She laughed. A moment later, Snaedis disappeared into the underground room.

Bryndis struggled to navigate the rope-ladder as it twisted and turned. When she'd finally made it down, she rested for a moment, leaning against a cement wall. Her aunt shone the flashlight slowly around the room and Bryndis followed the beam with her eyes. It was a drab grey color and the paint had almost entirely peeled off, but in one corner sat a large wooden desk in perfect condition. Behind it was a leather desk chair. On the wall above the desk was a framed oil painting of an elegant-looking gentleman in a military uniform.

"This is wonderful!" said Bryndis with awe. "I'm still shocked I never knew about this place. I wonder if Elena knew. Surely, if she did, she would have told me before she sold me the store. I'll have to call her."

Snaedis took a small, greenish-gold key out of her purse and headed to the desk. She opened up one of the large drawers, pulled out a Bible and handed it to Bryndis.

"Where'd you get the key?"

"Whoever knew about this place wasn't worried about security. I guess it was so hidden away, they didn't have to be. I found the key in the top desk drawer."

Bryndis held the Bible in her hands as if weighing it. It was the one that Holt had told her to hide. She'd never actually looked at it very carefully before. Holt had told her the box and the other things inside were "nothing," at the time, and that's the way she'd treated it. The Bible did look like nothing—the cover was black with white spots due to age, and there was a corner torn off. In faded letters, it said, *St. James Bible.* She turned to the first page and saw the initials, D.C. "Who do you think D.C. is?"

"Douglas Cole."

"Who's that?"

Snaedis got dreamy-eyed. "A hunky guy I dated in high school. Sorry, it was the first name I came up with."

"I still come back to the question," said Bryndis. "Why does everyone want this? What's so special about this particular Bible that all those men are willing to kill someone to get it?"

Snaedis shrugged, flopped down onto the wooden chair and aimed the flashlight beam onto the Bible so Bryndis could examine it.

Bryndis rifled through the yellowed pages, faded but still readable. She noticed that words on several of the pages had been underlined.

"Do you think these underlined words mean something?"

"I don't know. You could check it out with Jonathan."

"Jonathan?"

"You know, the guy who owns Rarities—the rare book store over in Vinson."

"Okay," said Bryndis, "but, first, let's get out of this cellar. It's creepy down here and now that I have the Bible, there's no reason to freeze ourselves to death down here."

The two women cautiously climbed their way back up the rope ladder and carefully replaced the wooden opening to the hidden cellar. It looked exactly as it had before. Just like part of the old wooden floor.

* * * * *

Later that day after she'd given her testimony to the police and after she'd gotten Frida settled in with Snaedis for a while, Bryndis stood in front of Jonathan J. Morgenstern, proprietor of Rarities. He was a short, puny man with long white hair that curled in all directions. His blue jacket was two sizes too large for him and his orange shirt had jam stains on it. Behind him, however, perfectly laid out in several glass counters, were numerous books, all numbered, and in plastic bags.

Mr. Morgenstern, with an eye piece in his right eye, closed the Bible. "It's authentic. I'll give you a hundred dollars."

Bryndis stared at him, puzzled. "That's all it's worth?"

He shrugged. "I've seen a few of these old St. James Bibles and most are in much better condition. Plus all this underlining lowers the value."

"It's initialed in the front—'D.C.'"

Morgenstern turned to the first page, and examined it closely. "Could be anyone." A distant look flashed into his eyes. "You know, I have this nutty friend named Theodore Schwitzle who's a Bible fanatic. He might be interested in this." He toyed with the book in his hands and then scratched something down on a scrap of paper from his pocket and handed it to Bryndis.

"What's this?"

"I thought you might want to talk to my nutty friend Theodore. This is his address."

Chapter Thirteen
by Patricia Rockwell

Bryndis headed home. As soon as she arrived, she plopped down on her bed and got out her address book to look up a number she hadn't called in a long time.

"Elena? Elena Vasquez?" she asked when a soft voice answered.

"Oh, my! Is this Bryn?" said the voice on the end of the line.

"Yes, Elena, it's me!" Bryndis was overjoyed to hear her mentor's voice. She felt a wave of guilt wash over her. How could she not have contacted her in these many years?

"How are you, dear? How is the shop? The building? How is your dear aunt, Snaedis? I think about you often."

"I'm fine; the shop is too. And so is Aunt Snaedis. I apologize for not having called you in so long. I'm afraid I have no excuse, but the strangest thing has happened that I thought you might want to know."

"Oh, my, what?"

"Elena, did you know that there was a cellar below the bookstore?"

"A cellar?" replied the old woman in a puzzled voice. "No. I thought the entire building was on solid ground. My father had had all of that remodeling done when I was a girl. Let's see that would have been in 1915 or so. My grandfather had owned the building as part of his farm, you know, which he sold, but he kept that building and eventually it was my father's idea to turn it into the center and divide it up into the four shops. I don't remember anything about a cellar. I always thought there was just dirt underneath."

"Well, it may be dirt under most of the building, but under The Neglected Word there's a small cellar—just a room, really. The entrance is through an opening in the wooden floor in the back room of the shop. You have to descend by a rope ladder. At the bottom, there's a small room, painted grey with an antique desk and a leather chair and an old oil painting of some soldier in uniform. That's all that's there, that I saw. Of course, I didn't really search it thoroughly."

"Oh, my, Bryn, that's extraordinary! I wonder what it's for. It sounds like it's been there for a long time."

"Yes," said Bryndis, "I would guess from the look of it that it was constructed that way originally. It obviously was intended to be secret. I wonder what it was for. Do you suppose any of your family knew about it?"

"Oh, dear, I don't know," replied Elena. "But, I will tell you what, Bryn. I'll see what I can find out. I have an older brother who might know something. Let me check with him and see if he has any idea what it was for—or even if he knows about it."

"Elena, that would be wonderful!" said Bryndis. "I'll call you soon." The two women exchanged some light family gossip, said their farewells and Bryndis pondered the information she'd just received.

Chapter Fourteen
by David M. Selcer

Rambler lounged in the back of his Volkswagen bus blowing smoke rings and listening to the Grateful Dead on his boom-box. Kiwa Campground was his permanent residence (for the month, that is), because it was the only RV Park near Harpshead that provided a public bathroom and a safe place to park his bike, but didn't require him to pay for a hook-up if he didn't want one. His neighbors scoffed when they passed his place, walking down the row to their Air Streams and Winnebago motor homes.

Not only was his the only VW bus in the park, but it was a 1971 VW with a pop-up top and sunflowers and naked women painted on the sides. Little felt balls hung down from strings adorning all the windows. A true moon wagon left over from the Woodstock generation, although Rambler was hardly old enough to have been at the greatest hippie fest of all time. His bus was the bane of Kiwa Trailer Camp. Residents sometimes left their bags full of garbage stacked beside it.

He was, however, oblivious to the derision of his neighbors. His bus had carried him all the way down the Pan-American Highway to Buenos Aires a few years ago. It had provided him with living quarters throughout his latest sojourn—a six month foray into Mexico that had taken him from San Antonio, Texas, to Cancun on the Yucatan peninsula.

Gradually, the marijuana Rambler was enjoying began taking its effect as he stared at the book-sized parcel lying on the bench seat along the inside wall of the other side of the van. What to do with it now that Holt was missing—that was the question. *Focus, focus.* Maybe that chick at Holt's apartment, claiming to be his girlfriend, or ex-girlfriend, or something like that, could help. Maybe he could get her to chill long enough to tell him where Holt might be. But how was he even going to find her? He didn't know where she lived. Maybe he could advertise in the local suburban newspaper. "Ex-hippie seeking important tête-a-tête with girlfriend, or former girlfriend, of Holt Furst. Call 555-753-4630." That would assume, of course, that he could keep his cell phone charged. It also might alert the others that something was up. Holt had cautioned him about the others. They coveted what Rambler had been sent to Mexico by Holt to get, and they'd stop at nothing to get it. Who were these people? Treasure hunters? Profiteers? Mobsters? Religious fanatics, who took the Bible literally—and believed that the cure to cancer was somewhere to be found in the Gospel of Luke? Some Wiccan group who wanted to resurrect the devil?

Whoever "the others" were, Holt had made it very clear that under no circumstances were they to have access to what Rambler had found in Mexico. Holt had made Rambler swear he'd never show it to anyone or discuss it with anyone. And he hadn't. Yet.

But how was he going to find Holt? Maybe he could just go back into town and post a note on Holt's door in case his buddy had finally made it back to his place. "Holt—call me dude. Rambler." Holt knew Rambler's cell number so he wouldn't have to put that in the note. That was an advantage. But what if Holt didn't make it back to his apartment? For all Rambler knew, Holt might be dead, compliments of "the others."

Then again, Rambler could always just go into town and ask around for Holt's woman. But that would certainly raise some questions he didn't want to discuss with anyone else. *Focus, dude, focus! Holt didn't pay all your expenses in Mexico just to provide a sunny vacation for you. You were supposed to find the code to that Bible and you found it. Now to get it to Holt. But how?*

He reached across the van to the white parcel containing the code book and opened it. Dusty and mildewed, the grey cloud that arose from the opened book mixed with the marijuana smoke. *Focus, dude, focus!*

This is a book about ancestors, read the first line. Then there was a family tree. Gabrial Gustave de Crocketaine was at the bottom—the base of the tree. Next came his son, Antoine de Saussure Peronette de Crocketaine, who was married to Louise de Saix, and there was a note that Antoine received a commission in the Household troops of Louis XIV of France, and a further note—*Immigrated to Ireland and changed family name to Crockett*. Their son, Joseph Louis, was born in Ireland and married Sarah Stewart; and then there was another note, this one saying—*Immigrated to New York*. Branching up from them were William David Crockett, born in 1709, who was married to Elizabeth Boulay. They had a son, David, born in Pennsylvania, who married Elizabeth Hedge. Above them were their six sons: William, David Jr., Robert, Alexander, James, Joseph and John, the last of whom was born in 1753 and married Rebecca Hawkins in 1780. Then one red line sprang up from John's name— David Crockett, born August 17, 1786.

The rest of the codex contained multiple facts about each of the family members mentioned therein, with an injunction that the family tree was to be placed in the prefatory pages of the Crockett family Bible by Congressman David Crockett, with whatever further facts he cared to include. It was signed by Piney, Boles and Pleath, Historians and Genealogists—London, March 4, 1835.

Rambler, who himself had been a history major at Northwestern University before his toking habit had begun turning his brain to jelly, knew that David Crockett, the last name in the genealogy, was none other than Davy Crockett himself—*King of the Wild Frontier*—Congressman Davey Crockett, pioneer Davey Crockett, woodsman Dave Crockett, and Davey Crockett, the soldier.

Through his travels in Mexico, Rambler had learned that this code book and a King James Bible had been taken from the body of Davy Crockett when he'd died at the Alamo in 1836 by one of the Mexican regulars who'd stormed the place. Rambler's research in Mexico had also revealed that, for a while, both books had been in the possession of General Antonio Lopez de Santa Anna, the great victor at the Battle of the Alamo during the Texas Revolution. It was rumored that the genealogy book Rambler now held contained a secret code which could only be deciphered by reading it in conjunction with this special King James Bible. The code, which Rambler had not yet broken, supposedly led to great hidden riches of Aztec gold that had been Santa Anna's secret stash. But try as he might, Rambler could discern no code from the genealogy/codex alone.

The "others" presumably knew about the codex, but did they know Rambler had it? Did they think he'd delivered it to Holt? How could they even know Rambler existed? The only people who knew about him were Holt, Holt's girl whom he'd met serendipitously at Holt's apartment, and some other guy who was with her there that day claiming to be Holt's little brother, Tony.

Voilà! That was it. He'd go into town tomorrow and find that Tony fellow who could probably help him track down Holt. Surely someone in Harpshead knew where he lived or worked. In the meantime, tonight he'd just let the pot stupor he'd gotten himself into carry him off into dreamland. Groggily, he took off his boots and put his feet up on the soiled couch. *To sleep, yet to dream—oh, sleep is coming fast.*

It must have been 4:00 in the morning when the side door of Rambler's van sliding back suddenly startled him out of his slumber. Rising too quickly, his head felt like someone had clamped a vice around his skull, forehead to back. It was the residue of THC from his partially dissipated pot session flooding his brain with adulterated oxygen as his heart pumped faster. What was that? Was there somebody standing in the van door? There was a bright light shining in from the street lamp outside that was literally useless in illuminating the figure silhouetted in the gaping entrance to the van. The dark shadow just seemed to hover there. Rambler rubbed his eyes, encouraging blood to engorge them. *Focus, focus—I must focus!*

"Rambler?" the figure said. "Rambler, it's me— Holt."

"That's what you say," Rambler said, wondering if he was dreaming. "But I can't see your face."

"Maybe this'll help," said the figure, illuminating his face with a flashlight that he shone up from his belt. The face was clear, unblemished and relaxed.

"Holt, my god! I thought you were—"

"Dead?" said the figure, completing Rambler's sentence.

"Well, I was at your apartment and—"

"I know," said the figure. "I wasn't there. I had to sort of evacuate quickly."

"Was it 'the others'?" Rambler asked, still groggy and fighting for clarity of mind.

"Yeah, the others. So do you have it?"

"Yah, yah," Rambler answered with pride. "I found the guy you bought the Bible from. He still had what he called *the key*, which I'm sure has to be the code book, but I can't make heads or tails of it."

"Lemme see it," Holt said. But there was something in his voice that gave Rambler pause. This wasn't the Holt he remembered. That Holt would have been much more laid back. He would have taken the time to ask how Rambler was—how the trip to Mexico was. He would have wanted to maybe blow a little pot before getting into the codex.

"What's the hurry, dude? You seem so uptight," Rambler replied. He looked at Holt's open shirt and jacket and noticed tattoos around his waist he'd never seen before. Something wasn't right. He knew Holt had read the Old Testament thoroughly and believed that body art was strictly forbidden. "Ye shall not make any cuttings in your flesh for the dead, nor print any marks upon you. I am the Lord your God."—Leviticus 19:28.

The two of them had discussed this many times, as Rambler had many tattoos to which Holt had always vigorously objected, even as he accepted most of Rambler's progressive life style. "You won't want to go back to your maker wearing all that vulgar decoration," Holt would say.

"Yes, but by the time I get there," Rambler would answer, "all this stuff will be decayed and my bones aren't marked up."

"So you're going to put one over on your maker, huh?" Holt would answer.

"Actually, I am a little uptight, Rambo," said Holt jovially as he now stood in the van's doorway. "I've just gotten out of the police station where they were holding me for questioning." The questioning had been all about why he'd been harassing Bryndis and what he'd been looking for in her apartment, but Rambler didn't need to know that—just as Rambler didn't need to know that his late night visitor was actually Holt's twin brother.

"So, hey, Holt," Rambler chided, "I see you're figuring on putting one over on your maker now too."

"Huh," Holt answered. "What are you talking about?"

Definitely, definitely, something isn't right here, Rambler figured. "You look just like Holt," he said, "and you sound just like him too, but how can I be sure you're Holt? I can't really see you very well in this light. But I know Holt didn't like tattoos, and you've got some."

"Just don't worry about it," Holt said. "Where's the codex?"

Rambler cast a furtive glance toward the opened white paper package on the couch across the van. And, that was it. Holt dove for the package and he grabbed it. Then he turned to leave, but Rambler snared his legs with a bull whip he kept by his cot that he'd brought back from Mexico as a souvenir, tripping him up and causing him to crash to the floor. "Not so fast," Rambler yelled. "I don't think you're really Holt. Let's see some ID."

Holt's twin brother—also known as Shadow—got up slowly and suddenly lunged at Rambler. The two of them became locked together in a sort of rolling combat all over the van. Cups and glasses came crashing down to the floor. Holt's brother grabbed a frying pan and began beating Rambler with it in the face. Rambler ran his hands over the other man's body to see if he had a gun. Then he found it, but not soon enough. Holt's brother was already drawing the weapon.

"What's going on in there, ya damn hippie?" came a voice from outside the van. "How are we supposed to sleep with that racket going on?" Three of Rambler's neighbors were standing outside his van in their pajamas, getting ready to enter.

Chapter Fifteen
by Lane Stone

"I object!"

Detective Krill rubbed his forehead, and leaned closer to the man opposite him at the wooden table. He lowered the volume and spoke slowly. The flower child, well beyond his sell-by date, seemed unperturbed.

"Mr. Rambler, or whatever your name is, we're in an interrogation room at the Harpshead Police Station, not a courtroom. You cannot object. Let's start over. The man you fatally shot in your van was named Holt?"

"Nah, man. That's what I'm objecting to. He *was* Holt, but he *wasn't* Holt."

"I'll need more than that. Who is this Holt?"

"Furst."

"First, what?" the detective asked.

"His last name." Rambler rolled his eyes, then winced at the pain. His attacker had gotten in a few good licks with that pan.

"What is Holt's last name?"

"Oh, my head." Rambler put his head in his hands, and pressed his palms against his forehead.

"Do you want to get checked out at the hospital? We can finish this later."

"Let's keep going. It's just that I can still see the look in his eyes when he knew he was about to buy it. Like I told you, I was asleep and he broke in and attacked me."

"Why did he target you? Why your van?"

Rambler shrugged his shoulders.

"If you don't mind my saying so," suggested Krill, "it didn't look like you had much to steal. Other than your motorcycle, which he could have gotten without even waking you up."

"Hey, my VW bus is classic."

"You can't think of what he might have been after?"

"No, idea."

"Maybe some of your, let's call it, agricultural imports?"

No way was Rambler answering that one. "Anyway, like I was sayin,' he broke in and we started fighting. He pulled a gun on me, but in the scuffle, he was shot."

There was a knock on the door and Krill got up to talk to a young uniformed officer. He handed the detective a paper and pointed to the middle of the page. This was just enough of a break to allow Rambler to finally see what he'd been trying so hard to get out of his head. The guy he'd killed was street tough, but Rambler was trained and, back in the day, had been disciplined. Both of their hands had been on the gun, pointed under *Holt's* chin. Rambler realized all he'd had to do was move his hand. And that's what he'd done. What the hell had his friend gotten him into?

"Mr. Rambler?"

"Yeah?" Rambler looked up at both officers, still standing at the open door.

"Why were we not able to find identification in your van? Not even a driver's license?"

"Don't know. Must have been stolen."

Rambler saw movement over Krill's shoulder out in the hallway. It was...what's-her-name? Holt's old girlfriend. The one he'd met when he'd gone to Holt's apartment that day. She was walking down the hall. He needed to talk to her. "Wait!" he yelled. She had her arm around a young girl, and she paused just long enough to see him and give him a look that said he'd have to improve to be an insect. He had to stop her, but how?

"Holt still loves you!" he yelled at her.

That stopped her in her tracks. She turned and gave him an almost imperceptible nod. Then she'd tightened her grasp around the young girl and walked on. *She'll talk to me*, Rambler thought to himself.

* * * * *

Bryndis sat behind the counter in her bookstore, warming her hands on a cup of tea. The sun was just coming up. Frida was asleep in Aunt Snaedis's apartment. The notes she'd made on Thursday, in what seemed like another lifetime, were spread before her. The number of pages made it painfully obvious that she had more questions than answers. Still the scribbles represented the last time she'd felt clarity, or control over her life.

She touched the line where she'd written about Tony saying he'd had class in half an hour and then later saying he'd had time to wait for the police. If she'd known that imposter wasn't Holt, why hadn't his own brother? They'd even hugged. She couldn't imagine not knowing someone was masquerading as Lia. Had Tony gotten mixed up in something? If he had, he was in way over his head.

She got up to toss her tea bag into the trash can and froze with her hand suspended over the trash bin. It reminded Bryndis of something else on her list: the chocolates that smelled so terrible, like bitter almonds, she suddenly realized. The bin had been emptied by the cleaning service, or by Aunt Snaedis. Any mystery lover worth her salt knew that the smell of bitter almonds indicated cyanide. *Who sent the candy?* she'd written on her list. She crossed out the word *sent*. The elegant red box hadn't been sent; it had been left by the door.

So what else had happened since Thursday when she'd started her notes? There was the introduction of Rambler. When had she started assuming he was with the criminals who'd kidnapped Holt and Frida? There was no evidence to support that. When she'd first seen him, he'd been trying to bring something to Holt. Her first thought when Detective Krill had told her about Rambler killing Holt's doppelganger, was that it was one less person to worry about. Now she saw it from a new angle. The Holt lookalike was their last connection to the kidnappers. How would they find Holt now—*if* he was still alive? Maybe Rambler could provide some information about Holt's whereabouts. She remembered seeing him in an interrogation room at the Police Station. He'd seen her too and had called out to her that Holt still loved her. Didn't that suggest that he knew Holt was still alive? After all, he'd just killed a spitting image of the man. She didn't know if or when Rambler would be released from police custody, but she resolved to try to contact him one way or another.

The oven timer pinged and she jumped. She was baking a batch of gluten-free brownies. As if on cue, the front door opened and Madge Miller and Bella Luchek walked in.

"So, is our favorite Charlotte Brontë fan still sleeping? Any chance she's starting to give Jane Austen a chance?" Bella's singsong voice rang through the bookstore.

"Cut the act, you two," Bryndis interrupted and slid the brownies toward the two ladies. "Detective Krill told me all about you being called out of retirement from the Missouri State Police for this case."

Over cups of tea, they told Bryndis how the State Police had come to a dead end in their investigation of a series of antiquities thefts. Bella and Madge had been called in to follow a man who looked like Holt, who called himself Shadow. A few months ago, he'd been parked outside Furst Fitness, and that's when the two women had spotted Holt too and realized that the two men must be twins. They'd been following both of them ever since and it had led them to what Holt called "the others" and the search for the mysterious Bible and its codex which ultimately led to Mr. Grey and his gang. That's what they were doing in the alley when they'd come across Elwin dragging Frida down that ramp. Everyone knew the story from there. Bella and Madge had just never revealed their true identities until now because they'd been working undercover and hadn't been given permission to reveal their true identities to anyone. Unfortunately, they couldn't tell Bryndis what she most wanted to know. Was Holt still alive?

This all started a few months ago? That coincides with Holt's personality change, thought Bryndis, *when the way he treated me changed so drastically.*

She came out of her thoughts when she heard the back door open. "Why did you let me sleep so long?" Frida called, yawning mid-sentence.

"You were up pretty late last night at the police station," Bryndis reminded her. "Look who's here!"

It was a joyous, if strange, reunion as Madge and Bella introduced themselves in their official capacity and explained their real reason for jumping in to save her from Grey's gang. Frida was delighted that the two old ladies were really the good guys and welcomed them both back with open arms. After all the explanations had been made, Frida spoke up.

"So, what's our next step, Aunt Bryn?" she asked.

Chapter Sixteen
by Jennifer Vido

The last thing Bryndis wanted to do was partake in a wild goose chase involving some rare book collector, but it seemed as if that was her only option for now. Jonathan Morgenstern at the Rarities Book Shop had been kind enough to warn her about his friend's rather eccentric tendencies. She figured it was his earnest attempt to excuse himself from any liability should the encounter prove futile. Bryndis could only imagine what danger she might be up against with the sought-after Bible in her possession. With Holt's twin brother out of the picture and the real Holt still missing, she realized the necessity of taking advantage of any viable leads. She wished Frida would have stayed safely behind with Aunt Snaedis, but her strong-minded niece rarely took no for an answer. The tell-tale bags under Bryndis's eyes betrayed her fear of successfully keeping Frida out of harm's way.

The drive to the nutty collector's home in nearby Vinson took less than fifteen minutes. It was an area of town Bryndis had passed through numerous times on her way to somewhere else. Regrettably, she'd never taken note of the surroundings...an oversight that could potentially have repercussions should danger arise. As for Frida, her unusually quiet demeanor signaled a red flag; however, Bryndis chose to linger a while longer with her own thoughts before dabbling in her niece's. She noticed Frida scribbling in a weathered notebook, most likely strategizing over Holt's whereabouts. As they turned the corner, Bryndis caught sight of the girl's elaborate drawings alongside columns of copious notes. Bryndis couldn't help but suppress a chuckle thinking of the difference between herself and her niece. She was never quite as inquisitive or creative as this child. Although they hadn't discussed it as of late, Bryndis sensed her niece was still disturbed by the fateful limo ride that had set this unfortunate chain of events in motion. She felt an obligation to her sister Lia to put an end to this nightmare before something bad happened to either one of them.

"Would you mind reading me this address, Frida Bonita? My eyesight is not what it used to be." She handed her niece the crumpled snippet of white paper. "If my navigational beacon is on target, we should be approaching the house at any minute. I tried to commit Mr. Morgenstern's directions to memory, but it was hard keeping up with him. That man talked so fast!"

Frida squinted and hesitated before responding, "I think it says 302 Greenway, but I'm not certain. Mr. Morgenstern's handwriting is illegible. Typical man!" They chuckled at her honest observation. "So, what's our plan, Aunt Bryn?" Her intense gaze conveyed a vested interest in the rendezvous.

Bryndis paused for a moment and then replied, "I think it's best if we let him do the talking. Let's pretend we're sponges. Soak up as much information as we can without leaking any important clues about the case. Got it?" Bryndis's animated hand motions prompted Frida to mirror her liveliness by heartily nodding in agreement and clapping her hands.

"296, 298 …we're getting closer," Frida said with an air of excitement. Her enthusiasm quickly took a nosedive when they rolled up to a dank, dark brown split-level abode with a tarnished metal mailbox. Affixed to its side were faded black stickers. "Does that say 302? Aunt Bryn, do you think anyone actually lives here?"

Bryndis concentrated on parking the car as close to the curb as possible before responding to Frida. She needed some extra time to choose her words carefully. Taking a deep breath, she sputtered, "I'm not surprised at all. This man Theodore Schwitzle is a rare book collector who probably spends every waking hour with his nose in a book. Clearly, he concentrates all his energies on his hobby rather than his home. Just the kind of man we're looking for. I have no doubt he'll help us figure out why this Bible is so important." Bryndis didn't allow her own insecurities to taint Frida's thoughts. The smile on Frida's face indicated a job well done.

The two slowly emerged from the vehicle with their eyes wide open, taking note of the overgrown shrubbery and decrepit chain-link fence. Bryndis adjusted her frumpy purse with the Bible neatly tucked inside and then grabbed her niece's hand. In any situation other than the present, Frida would have adamantly rejected her motherly overture. It was plain to see they needed one another now though. Bryndis sensed the vibe emitting from the palm of the girl's hand was one of pure fright.

It took less than ten paces before they were standing squarely in front of a dilapidated wooden door. Adorned with cobwebs, dust, and dirt, it did not show signs of regular usage. Gathering her courage, Bryndis leaned forward and pushed the rectangular doorbell. No sign of movement or the sound of footsteps. She tried again with no luck. Frida shrugged her shoulders and then motioned to Bryndis to knock. With all the strength she could muster, Bryndis beat rat-a-tat-tat on the heavy door, producing the desired results.

The creaking sound of the door opening caused the pair to retreat a few steps. The fear of the unknown got the better of them but they were surprised when they were greeted by a strapping, six-foot tall gentleman with slicked back salt and pepper hair and a mustache. Attired in a designer sports coat, khaki slacks, and Italian loafers, his appearance did not match his meager surroundings. His soothingly mellow voice invited the pair to come inside while exchanging introductions and handshakes.

"Hello, I'm Theodore Schwitzle. Jonathan said you'd be dropping by. I'm glad you were able to find my home. I keep meaning to replace the worn-out house numbers on the mailbox, but I seem to get sidetracked more times than not." His warm smile was intended to chase away any doubts Bryndis and Frida may have had. From the looks of things, it was going to take more than just a flashy grin to calm their jittery nerves.

As if on cue, he ushered Bryndis and Frida into the dim living room while doing his best to engage them in idle chit-chat. Motioning towards two comfy-looking club chairs, he encouraged them to make themselves at home while he fetched cold drinks. The two politely obliged.

It didn't take long for Bryndis's eyes to soak up the sheer magnitude of the room. Each of the four walls contained bookcases overflowing with well-read volumes of classic literature. Heavy rust and orange-checked drapes kept the sunlight at bay as exquisite pieces of antique furniture rested on a notable blood-red Persian rug. A sole, lit candle high on a shelf emitted a hint of light. Frida, on the other hand, zeroed in on a tiny calico cat nesting in a basket of multi-colored yarn. She was clearly preoccupied with the cute bundle of fur rather than taking in the peculiar surroundings.

"I hope you two ladies like lemonade, seeing as that's the only sugary beverage I may offer you today. If you prefer water, of course, I do have that, too. You caught me on my way out to the grocery store. I'm afraid my cupboard and refrigerator are bare to the bone." Schwitzle returned and presented three tall glasses filled with ice and lemonade on a beautifully hand-painted serving tray. He passed each one of them a cocktail napkin accompanied by a refreshing beverage. He set the tray on a nearby side table and proceeded to help himself as well.

Bryndis noticed the humorous saying printed on the square napkin...*A friend will make you lemonade. A true friend will add vodka.* A nonchalant whiff of the beverage confirmed it safe for imbibing. Not one to mince words, she began, "So, I have this Bible..."

"So I hear." Schwitzle cocked his left eyebrow in retort.

"Well, um, it's not my Bible. It belongs to a friend."

A dubious grin adorned Schwitzle's face. "Isn't that always how the story goes?"

Bryndis and Frida exchanged a look of surprise.

Schwitzle kicked back and planted his feet on an adjacent ottoman. He then proceeded to twirl the swizzle stick in his beverage. Evidently, lemonade was not all that he was drinking.

Bryndis tried a different approach. "What sparked your interest for collecting rare books?" Schwitzle's eyes immediately lit up. "Your collection is mighty impressive." She waved her hand about, circling the room.

As expected, Schwitzle delighted in talking about his favorite topic...himself. For the next fifteen minutes, he traced his journey of book collecting, highlighting his most prized acquisitions in his collection. At times, it seemed as if he was lost in his own reverie while reminiscing about some unfortunate disappointments along the way. Just when it seemed like the story was heading towards a climax, he got sidetracked on a tirade about some kooky philosopher. It was at that point, Bryndis decided to cut him off.

"So, getting back to why we're here, this Bible I have with me contains some initials inscribed in the front...D.C. Any chance you might know what these letters stand for?" Bryndis slipped the book out of her purse and handed it over to Schwitzle.

Like any true rare book collector, Schwitzle handled the specimen carefully. While holding it gently in his left hand, he removed a folded handkerchief from his pants pocket with his right hand. He spread the hankie across his lap and then proceeded to place the book on top of it. Next, he withdrew a magnifying glass from the inside pocket of his sport coat. Page by page, he evaluated the Bible before him, making only slight grunts and *ums* as he perused the manuscript. Five minutes must have passed before anyone spoke.

"Does the cat go outside?" Frida asked. She had positioned herself right next to its basket, careful not to disturb the innocent creature.

Both Bryndis and Schwitzle were taken aback. Her previous silence had almost caused them to forget she was in the room.

Schwitzle simply responded, "No," and then continued his evaluation.

Bryndis passed the time biting her nails and checking her cell phone for text messages.

"In my opinion," Schwitzle finally said, "this is a rare edition. Truly valuable, even with the markings like so. Where did you find this book?"

"The logistics are neither here nor there. What matters is the Bible and its value, wouldn't you say?"

The look in Schwitzle's eyes sent shivers down Bryndis's spine. All of a sudden, the mood in the room shifted. Schwitzle was silent, focusing all of his energy on the book in his possession. Bryndis noticed him tightening his grasp on the Bible. He then reached inside the drawer of the side table and pulled out a handgun.

Bryndis bolted up out of her seat. "Frida, look at the time! We almost forgot about your ballet lesson. Good thing you thought ahead and packed your bag in the car. We won't have time now to stop back home and change." Bryndis eyed her niece, giving her a signal that trouble loomed.

Before they had a chance to consider grabbing the book and dashing away, their tête-à-tête came to a sudden halt when the sound of a familiar voice came through the front door.

"Not so fast, ladies. I figured I'd find you here."

Chapter Seventeen
by Diane Weiner

Bryndis's jaw dropped. Frida gasped. There in the doorway with a gun in his hands, stood Holt's brother, Tony.

"They fell right into our trap, Tony," said Schwitzle. "Like flies to honey, wrapped and delivered. They even came bearing a gift." Schwitzle cradled the Bible in his arms like a newborn baby.

"Oh, no, Tony!" cried Bryndis. "Not you!" She hugged Frida. Tony remained unmoved, gun still firmly aimed in their direction.

"Oh my God!" said Frida, now pointing at Schwitzle. "That's...that's...the man who kidnapped me. That's Mr. Grey!" She took a step backward.

Schwitzle broke into the English accent he'd had the first time Frida had met him.

"Allow me to properly introduce myself." He put down the Bible and extended one hand while holding the gun in the other. "Nathan Grey—or, at least, that's one of my names."

Now Frida could see it. He'd disguised himself by adding streaks of color in his hair, and a fake mustache. The room where she'd first met him had been dark and Frida hadn't been able to see him well—just his eyes. She recognized those piercing eyes now. And she hadn't really scrutinized him when they first arrived today. She'd been more interested in the cuddly calico sitting in the basket.

Schwitzle—or Grey—or whoever he was— chuckled. "Maybe you should have been reading some Lemony Snicket instead of Brontë, my dear Frida. Seems as if you've fallen into a series of unfortunate events." He turned to Tony. "Take care of these complications straight away. After the task is complete, lock this Bible in my vault." He gave the Bible a kiss before letting it go.

"Yes, sir," said Tony. He continued to point the gun at Bryndis and led her and Frida to the dark sedan parked outside. Bryndis simply could not believe this was Tony standing here, pointing a gun at her. Tony, whom she'd known since he was a teenager. She shuddered. How could she have been so wrong about him?

"Get in," said Tony. Bryndis and Frida scooted into the car. When they'd driven out of sight from the house, Tony began to explain.

"You're in no danger. Sorry for the charade." Tony's voice softened. "I'm an undercover detective, believe it or not."

"What?" said Bryndis. Had she fallen through the looking glass? How could this day get more bizarre?

"After I graduated from Eastern Missouri," explained Tony, "I decided to apply to the police academy. After all, I was holding a BA in English with no job offers in sight. I'd always been interested in police work, so applying to the academy seemed like a palatable option."

"Why would you keep that a secret?" asked Bryndis. "We all would have been proud of you."

"Because shortly after entering the academy," he said, "I was flagged as a potential undercover detective. They were trying to break a drug ring and because I looked so young, they figured I could fit in with the dealers. I was placed at the local high school as a substitute teacher to gather information. Lots of drug deals go down at high schools."

Bryndis scratched her head. "Then how did you get from undercover drug dealer to working for that heinous criminal we just left?"

"The situation simply presented itself. The police had been tracking Grey for years. He specializes in stealing rare works of art and literature. It was when I first started subbing. This guy approached me and asked if I wanted to make some cash. There was a load of stolen paintings that needed to be transported. He figured a substitute teacher could use the money. As it turned out, he was one of Grey's thugs. This was too good of an opportunity for the department to pass up."

"Wait 'til I tell my Mom about this!" said Frida. Her voice was more animated than Bryndis had ever heard. Bryndis wondered if she was actually enjoying this. Tony drove for what seemed like an eternity. He exited onto a dirt road that led up to a log cabin.

"Here we are," he said. "This is one of the department's safe houses. You and Frida have to lay low here for a while. Grey has to believe that I killed you."

"How long do we have to stay here?" Bryndis asked.

"Hopefully, not long," replied Tony, "but if you go back home now, Grey will no doubt find out and you won't be safe and my true identity will be revealed too soon."

The cabin smelled like a mixture of newly cut pine and dust. Tony cracked a window and turned on the dim floor lamp near the sofa. Then he handed the Bible back to Bryndis with instructions to keep it safe.

"What's so important about this Bible? Why does Grey want it so badly?"

"It's a long story. Holt was inadvertently given the Bible while vacationing in Mexico. His instincts told him it was something valuable—something with a history. When he returned to the States, he did some research and uncovered quite the story. Apparently, this Bible, in conjunction with a codex—in actuality a book of the Crockett family genealogy—was stolen from Davy Crockett's dead body by an aide to the Mexican General Santa Anna at the Alamo back in 1836."

"Okay, I'm not following this at all," said Frida.

"I'll cut to the chase. Legend has it that reading both books together gives the location of a stash of Aztec gold. This gold would be worth a fortune today. That's why Grey wanted to get his hands on both books—the Bible and the codex."

"Maybe we can crack the code ourselves and get our hands on the gold," suggested Frida. At the moment, Bryndis thought her niece sounded less like Jane Eyre and more like Nancy Drew.

"No, I'm pretty sure that the gold—if it actually exists—belongs to the Mexican government," said Bryndis.

"Well, we could still work on cracking the code. We'll have time," suggested Frida.

"Yes, you will," said Tony. "But it probably won't do you much good, Bryn, if you don't have the codex. But good luck. Many, as they say, have already tried and failed. I'm going to continue to hunt down the codex anyway. I'm pretty sure that hippie we saw at Holt's apartment has it. That guy who was posing at Holt attacked him and Rambler killed him in self-defense."

"Oh no!" cried Bryn. "He's dead?"

"Yeah," said Tony, "but the cops called it self-defense and released Rambler, so I'm pretty sure he's taken his flower power van and skipped town. He seemed like our best lead in finding Holt."

After Tony left, Bryndis and Frida went to work trying to crack the code in the Bible. After hours trying to transpose various underlined words, they were about to give up for the night. Frida stifled a yawn, and Bryndis rubbed her tired eyes. Her head was hurting. Then Frida had a light bulb moment.

"Aunt Bryn, I just thought of something. Maybe this has something to do with that note you found in Holt's apartment. Remember? Booth 153."

"We explored that lead already and it was a dead end. That crazy man in the yellow hat didn't know anything and there was no one at that booth."

"Maybe we misinterpreted the note. Maybe 153 stands for something else."

Frida hurriedly turned to page 153 in the Bible, but it was another dead end. Then they tried circling words in the pattern of first, fifth, and third words on each page. That proved to be equally frustrating. All of a sudden, Frida's eyes lit up with excitement. "It's a Bible, Aunt Bryn. What do you think of when you put together a number and the Bible?"

"You mean a Bible verse?" said Bryndis. "Or maybe a Psalm number. I'll bet that's it." They turned to Psalm 153. "This verse was spoken by David after he slayed the lion and the wolf. He was giving thanks to God for saving him."

She read: *Look on my suffering and deliver me for I have not forgotten your law*—Psalm 153.

"What do you think it means, Aunt Bryn? Do you think it has something to do with the Alamo and Texas trying to get independence from Mexico? There was a lot of suffering at the Alamo. After all, Holt received the book in Mexico."

Bryndis thought and said, "It might." She flipped through the book and her face broke into a wide smile. "It might."

Chapter Eighteen
by Sharon Rose

Rain pattered gently on the roof. The cabin was dark now. Frida slept. Bryndis was exhausted but thoughts raced through her mind. Perhaps she was being carried away with the whole idea. Who would really believe that if you put an old Bible and some kind of codebook together, a person could find a treasure? And yet, it seemed people were ready and willing to murder for these relics. Why would they know to target her? How would they know she had the Bible when she didn't even know at the time? Why didn't they just break into her shop when she wasn't there? No one needed to kill her. In fact, she would gladly have handed over anything she'd found.

Bryndis's mind was in overdrive. Her mother had always told her that she had a great imagination and it was obvious her niece carried some of those genes. When she'd looked at Frida and seen the dark circles around her eyes, she knew her niece didn't need any more stimulus—she needed sleep. This was proven true because in less than a minute, the young girl had fallen sound asleep.

Not only that, she wondered about the history of her shop. With that hidden cellar, what stories might it tell? Elena had told her some things, but she obviously didn't know that much. She remembered Elena saying that the building was over two hundred years old. She recalled that it once had been part of a large farm or plantation. What today were the four shops were at one time quarters for farm workers.

"Just what's hidden inside that Bible?" she said aloud. She slapped her hand over her mouth for speaking aloud and looked at her niece. Frida slept on.

She turned the light on before walking over to the table where the old Bible lay.

"Imagine," she whispered, as she caressed the cover. "Davy Crockett held this book just like I am." Then, straightening up, she said, "Well, maybe he did. Who knows?" One thing she knew for sure; she felt better when she talked to herself, and as long as she didn't wake the sleeping girl, she would keep doing it.

She snuggled down into the comfortable chair, rearranged the light, and started to search. She slowly perused the Bible, page by page, taking note of each underlined word or phrase. Unfortunately, there were simply too many words to contemplate. After half an hour and getting nowhere, she decided she needed something to keep her awake.

Bryndis went into the kitchen. She opened the refrigerator door. Whoever had stocked the fridge was not going to let them starve. She next opened the door to a small pantry. There was enough food for at least a month. Surely, they wouldn't have to stay that long? She walked back to the fridge and pulled out a Coke. What she really needed was a hot cup of coffee, but she was afraid brewing sounds would wake up Frida.

Sipping on the cold drink, she sat back into the big soft chair. She thought again about the note she'd found at Holt's apartment that said Booth 153. Was it just a coincidence that there was a Booth 153 at The Midwest Book Lovers' Convention? Why would Holt make a note about that? The man who never read a book in his life, much less attended a book fair.

"I wish my mother would've been stricter with me about learning Bible verses," she mumbled as she continued to scan the pages.

"Aunt Bryn?" Frida sat up, eyes wide. "Is there someone here? Please, tell me we're safe."

Bryndis rushed over and held her. "I'm sorry, sweetie. Did I wake you? I got carried away talking to myself." She held Frida's face in her hands. "Don't worry, we're safe, and soon you'll be back home." She laughed. "Although it might be a long time before your mother sends you my way again."

Frida giggled. "Well, I don't think we have to give Mom all the details, Aunt Bryn."

Bryndis gave her another hug. "Go back to sleep. I'm shutting the light off now. I'll be right here in the chair across from you."

Bryndis shut the light off and by the time she settled into the chair, Frida was asleep again. It was raining harder now and there was no moonlight shining in. She could hear the wind howling around the corners of the cabin and branches scratching against the window.

If only Holt were here. She'd tell him about the secret room. What had it been used for? And that painting? Who was the soldier in that painting? It didn't look like her memory of what Davy Crockett looked like. And what, if anything, did the painting—or the secret cellar have to do with any of this?

And somewhere out in the storm, she thought she heard voices.

Chapter Nineteen
by Drema Reed

"Ow. Ow!"

"Be quiet or the whole world will know we're sneaking up on them."

"I told you not to come this way. It's too dark. If you'd just listened to me—"

"Oh, yeah, because that worked out so well the last time."

"Well, it wasn't my fault that guy was standing outside the door with a gun." Madge pushed a tree branch out of her face and pellets of rain fell down on her head.

Bella trudged on, ignoring the fact that her shoes were now soaking wet and a squishing sound was coming from her feet. Madge was still mumbling something that Bella was sure she didn't want to hear right now, so she ignored her too.

The house was a good half mile off the main road and completely surrounded with bushes, making it nearly impossible—if not completely impossible—to get a good look through the windows. There was no way to know what was going on inside or who was doing the going on. Perhaps just an old-fashioned frontal approach would have been more effective. Sometimes just a good hard knock on the door provided more access than peeking through the windows. However...

Deciding it wouldn't hurt to try and just get a peek, Bella had stopped suddenly outside one of the larger windows, causing Madge to plow into her, knocking them both "backside over tea kettle" into the bushes, causing a hell of a racket. The bushes scraped across the screens, Bella had let out with a string of swear words that turned the air blue, and Madge was sure she was going to get shot. And what with all the thunder and lightning from the storm, probably no one other than the shooter would hear it.

"We're going to die!" wailed Bella. "Madge, it's all your fault."

"It's always my fault. Why should this occasion be any different?" Madge replied. She had managed to right herself, offered a helping hand to Bella—who would have ignored it if she'd thought she could get up on her own—and pulled her to her feet. Pieces of branches from the bushes were stuck in Bella's hair; Madge had mud up to her ankles and they were both soaking wet. The two of them stood there, trying to decide which of them looked the worst and then burst into laughter. What the heck? No one had shot at them so far.

"Okay," said Madge, pushing her stringy wet hair out of her face, "let's just go and knock on the door. We can always say we got lost walking in the woods. Maybe at least this will give us a chance to see who's in there."

"Good idea. Maybe they have a few towels and we can dry off." Bella was so practical when it came to creature comforts.

Throwing caution to the already blowing wind, they made their way up the stairs and Madge knocked on the door. Not knowing what fate awaited them, Bella had her over-sized umbrella in striking position. (Why she'd failed to open it when it was needed to keep the rain off them, Madge had no idea. Sometimes Bella was just

Bella and there was no sense in trying to ascertain her motives.)

Bryndis had been getting used to the branches scraping against the windows as the wind was blowing fiercely, continually knocking one against the other. When she heard an especially loud sound, she reached over and turned on the table lamp. *Is someone out there?* The glow from the small bulb threw the room into a relief of shadows along with the dying fire, and after looking around, deciding she was being silly, she reached for the light. Before she could turn it off, a loud knock sounded at the door. Bryndis flew from her chair and Frida sat straight up out of a sound sleep.

"What's happening?" Frida asked, trying to shake away the fog of sleep.

"Someone's at the door," Bryndis answered nervously. "No one knows we're here except Tony." She was trying to reassure herself as well, as she picked up the fireplace poker and cautiously made her way to the door, Frida close on her heels.

"Who's there?" called Bryndis, her voice shaking more than she would have liked.

"It's us! Madge and Bella. Let us in please. It's wet out here."

Bryndis threw open the door and there they stood—two old ladies, soaked to the bone, wet hair hanging in their faces, one with an umbrella hoisted over her head, just in case. Just in case what, no one was sure. *Be prepared* came to mind.

"Oh, my," interjected Frida, peeking around Bryndis. "You ladies look terrible."

"Don't be vague, young lady," bellowed Bella. "Tell us how we really look. And by the way, Frida, I took to heart your advice to ask, 'What would Jane do?' Only in my case, it wasn't Jane Eyre or Jane Austen, it was

Jane Fonda. She did some pretty outrageous things, you know."

"Could we cut this conversation and jump to the part where you let us in?" said Madge, getting tired of all the rhetoric and being more than a little cranky.

"Oh, I'm so sorry," said Bryndis, embarrassed by her lack of hospitality. "Of course, please come in. Frida get some towels from the linen closet. Bella, Madge, take off your wet coats and put them over here by the fire so they can dry. Your shoes too," she added, looking at the wet puddles on the floor. "I'll make some tea," she said, moving into the kitchen area, filling the kettle and turning on the stove. "You must be cold on top of everything else."

"Yeah," offered Madge. "On top of everything else!"

Frida did as she was told and handed each of the ladies a towel to dry their hair and faces. They removed their coats and shoes, placing them on the chairs Bryndis had supplied near the fire and dried their hair. Once they'd finished, they lowered themselves onto the sofa and both let out huge sighs of relief.

While Bryndis fiddled in the kitchen, gathering cups and saucers, Frida found she couldn't contain herself any longer and questions started pouring forth from her mouth like tennis balls from an electric ball machine. "What are you doing here? How did you find us? How come you're so wet if you have an umbrella with you?"

"You want to take this one?" said Madge, giving Bella a look that was more than a bit accusatory. "Why, indeed, are we so wet if we had an umbrella with us?"

"That's irrelevant," answered Bella with a wave of her hand, as if knocking the question into oblivion where it belonged.

Bryndis returned with a tray filled with cups, a tea pot, sugar and milk, and then poured a cup for each of them. She settled back in her chair, gave the two women a questioning look and waited for some answers. After a few moments of silence, Madge relented and provided Bryndis and Frida with answers.

"We followed you two to that creepy-looking house down on Greenway and waited in the car, just in case you needed help or something. We watched as some character drove up, got out of the car and went inside the house. The next thing we knew, he brought you two out at gun point and loaded you into his car."

"Yeah," agreed Bella, "And we, being the astute detectives that we are, figured a guy pointing a gun at you probably was some kind of a clue in this Bible mystery you're involved in, so we followed you out here. When he turned in the driveway, we waited there until we saw him leave a few minutes later. We didn't know if you were in here alone or if someone was holding you hostage. That's the reason we look so ridiculous. We tried to peek in the windows and fell into the bushes."

"Now, our turn," said Madge as she set her cup down on the coffee table. "Who is that guy who brought you here? Who was in the house on Greenway and why is everybody running around like a bunch of chickens with their heads cut off participating in some kind of a treasure hunt? I know you told us about a Bible. We know about the gangsters who tried to kidnap Frida, and we know about Booth 153, but how does this all fit together? It would be nice to know we'd nearly drowned ourselves for some glorious reason."

"Other than stupidity," added Bella.

"Other than that," agreed Madge.

Bryndis blew out a puff of air between pursed lips, set her cup down alongside Madge's, and proceeded to explain as best she could what was going on, ending with an explanation of who Tony was and how he'd brought them to this safe house, along with the Bible.

"Some safe house," said Bella snidely. "Two old ladies found you without even trying very hard."

Bryndis turned to Frida, gave her an apologetic look and told the story of the Bible, the code book, the secret room below her shop, along with her speculations of how it all might tie together and lead to a mysterious treasure.

"Aunt Bryn," exclaimed Frida. "Why didn't you tell me about all this? A secret room! How delicious! You have secrets no one knows about! But then," she said, frowning a little, "I guess that's what being a secret is all about, isn't it? No one knows about it."

"I didn't want to say anything because I'm not sure," Bryndis said. "All I know is that Mr. Grey really wants this Bible—which I have now! He also needs the codebook and we don't know where that is, but I can't help but think there might be a clue in the secret cellar. I mean, that cellar has been untouched for years, maybe decades. Who knows what might be hidden there? Maybe there really is a clue to the codebook's whereabouts down there. Maybe that's why Holt got involved in the first place. I just don't know. Good Lord, where could he be? Sorry, Frida. I know you like to be in on things. Maybe the person who left me that poisoned candy wants me dead because they want to get into the secret room. Maybe there's something there of value and we just don't realize it and whoever it is figures if I'm gone, they'll be free to investigate the room."

"So," said Bella, chin in her hand, elbow on her knee, "the bottom line here is we need to get into that secret room, and apparently the sooner the better. Those bad guys are still out there trying to find you two and this Bible, so we need to be secretive ourselves."

"Yes," sighed Bryndis. "But how are we going to do that? It's raining cats and dogs, Tony would not be happy if we just left here and, most important, we don't have a way to get there. We don't even have a car."

"Yes, you do!" said Madge, jumping up from her seat on the couch. "*We* have a car, *ergo, you* have a car. Let's get out of here and be on our way. We can tell Tony later. We'll keep you both safe. Get dressed, you two, and don't forget your rain boots." She'd pulled Bella's arm and yanked her off the couch, causing the older woman to lose her balance and fall with a 'wop' back onto the couch.

"Come on, Bella. Let's go!" commanded Madge, the decibel level in her voice rising now to levels too high for any small critters lurking nearby. Bella stared at her with a glower, but didn't move.

"What? Do you need me to rearrange the word order in that sentence? Come on, all of you! Let's get the heck out of here and go check out that cellar."

They got the heck out of there.

Chapter Twenty
by Amy Beth Arkawy

The quirky quartet of sleuths made good time as they navigated the slick roads and brutal winds en route to Bryndis's shop and the coveted secret room. They didn't notice the unwelcome trio of tailgaters following them until they parked in the lot behind The Neglected Word.

"Shiitake mushrooms!" Bella blurted as she exited the car and saw three men bolt out of a luxury sedan behind them with guns drawn.

"Oh, God! This can't be good," Bryndis whispered as she spied Mr. Grey—or Schwitzle. She wrapped her arm tightly around Frida, just as her brave niece let out a gasp.

"Damn! How did he—?" Madge was ashen.

"GPS tracking. You think we'd let you roam around playing Miss Marple and her addled older sister without one?" Mr. Grey, his English accent fading in and out, punctuated his remark with a bitter snicker.

"Who exactly is supposed to be Miss Marple's *addled* older sister?" exclaimed Bella, manipulating the umbrella and getting it set for action.

"Open the door," ordered Mr. Grey. "Do it now!"

Bryndis was shaking, fumbling for her keys as she made her way to her store's door. Frida, numb from shock, stuck to her side.

"Not so fast!" Madge said in harsh, no-nonsense tones again. "We need to establish ground rules first."

"Never mind ground rules," said Grey. "It's raining like crazy canaries. We need to get inside pronto."

"Oh, for God's sake, Bella, open that monstrosity already. It could cover all of us," Madge sniped.

"I don't think you're exactly in any position to give orders, Magpie." Mr. Grey moved closer to Madge, flashing a seductive smile.

"Magpie?" Bella's mouth hung agape.

"But I am, Greysie."

"Greysie? What? You two are—" Bella, unsteady on her tired feet, leaned against the wall, inadvertently knocking over a sandwich board listing specials that Bryndis's Aunt Snaedis must have forgotten to bring inside. *Hot Cross Buns* may have been as appropriate as they were scrumptious. And *The Talented Mr. Ripley,* Patricia Highsmith's riveting portrait of a murderous sociopath living a double life flashed a big neon warning sign in Bryndis's overloaded mind.

"Is your name really Grey? I thought it was Schwitzle…uh, none of my business," Frida demurred, clinging to Bryndis.

"I told you that one was sharp," Madge said and smiled, tapping Bella on her shoulder.

"You told me after I told you, Mrs. I've Got Lots of 'Splaining to Do."

"Either way, she's a smart girl," Madge smiled. "Truth is, he has so many aliases, he's forgotten his real name. Isn't that right, Greysie?"

"But Grey is Magpie's favorite," Grey said, offering a benign grin as he rubbed Madge's shoulders.

Had they been double-crossed by—of all people— Madge? Bryndis's mind was reeling back to that horrible scene with Holt's doppelganger. He had waved his gun with such a wretched expression, so alien to the sweet Holt she'd known so well for so long. *Oh, Holt.* Bryndis could feel her eyes well up with tears. *No time for that now.* That cruel fraud had unnerved Bryndis so, she'd forgotten some of the claims he'd made as he tried to wrangle his way out of trouble. He'd said, "Don't listen to them." *They're with the gang. One is even married to one of them. Could it be? Is Madge, the sweet old retired state detective, a double agent? Is she really mixed up in this murderous mess? Is she actually married to Grey?*

"This is not how it was supposed to go down," Madge said with a weary sadness in her eyes. "No one was supposed to get hurt. You had it all planned out. You're always so careful."

"Well, plans go awry, love. Too many moving parts in this one. And some had low IQs." Grey shrugged as he continued Madge's massage.

Bryndis and Frida looked at Bella who shook her head. "No idea. Absolutely none. You better fill us in, Madge, before I get accused of being an accomplice. Guilt by association has landed more than a few convicts in the clink. I should know. I locked up my share."

"Oh, cripes, Bella. You're like a broken record with your jailbird phobia. Go binge watch *Orange is the New Black* and be done with it already." Madge sighed, swatting Grey's hands away like she would overstuffed mosquitoes punch drunk on eating revelers at a sultry summer party.

"I may have a phobia but it will be your reality soon," whined Bella.

"Not necessarily. Greysie and I can still make a clean break. I have my heart set on that hammock in Tahiti." Madge cocked her head and signaled her honey's henchmen.

Bryndis was shocked when the tough guys stowed their guns in their coats on Madge's command. Did Madge really wield that much power? Was she the brains of the operation? Bella's mammoth umbrella had finally risen to the occasion, protecting everyone from the rain, at the exact moment Bryndis got her key in the shop's door.

"Perfect timing, Bella. As usual," Madge snipped, as they all filed in like the Seven Dwarves. But there was no whistling. Just grumbling and nerves. Bryndis was comforted, for a sweet moment, by her familiar sanctuary, the smell of books and pastry. *Home, finally.* But not exactly on her own terms. Still, she hugged Frida close and whispered, "It'll be okay. It's almost over."

"A fine bit of fiddle-faddle," Bella grumbled. "What gives, Madge? I deserve the whole story. How and why did you get mixed up in all of this?"

"The short version, Magpie. We don't have time for Memory Lane," Mr. Grey said. "We're here on serious business."

"Two years ago, during that Washington University gallery heist. You were on the *DL* with cataract surgery, Bella, and I was paired with that dolt, Eddie Swayze."

"Eddie Swayze? He's a matinee idol. Well, an aging matinee idol. Always was a little sweet on me." Bella, beaming, was still maneuvering her umbrella, trying to get it to close and be primed for instant weaponry.

"He's an old fool," continued Madge. "Anyway, that's when I met Snuggie."

"Snuggie?" responded Bella. "Oh, dear Lord, you are over the edge."

"What can I tell you? The heart wants what it wants," Madge sighed. "You know everyone thinks I'm an old bag because I run around with Bella. But there's a big difference between 81 and 67. I'm still a vibrant woman with real needs. I got groovy with Arlo Guthrie at Woodstock, for God's sake. I just dress like a frump to throw everyone off." Madge pulled on her latest sack dress, this one a garish printed blouse ordered on clearance from the Home Shopping Channel. "Old ladies are invisible. That's a very powerful tool." She nodded at Frida. "It works for young women, too. As I recall."

"That's rich," Bella scoffed. "So now you have one of those fool-proof memories like Marilu-What's-Her-Name, all of a sudden?"

Madge shook her head and chuckled. "Oh, Bella, you're still a doozy."

"Okay, we're all caught up, right?" Grey's steely eyes were fixated now on Bryndis. "I believe you have something to show us, young lady."

"I don't. I mean I don't know." Bryndis swallowed hard, alarmed to discover her throat felt as if it was covered in wet gravel. She wasn't sure what to do. Should she open the secret hatch and just let the gang have their way with whatever was down there? *That makes some sense*, she thought. But what if there was nothing of value there? No clue? What if they came up empty? Would that put her and Frida in more danger? *Oh, God, Frida.* She had to protect her precious niece.

"No one will get hurt," Madge said again in her most severe voice. "That much I can guarantee."

"Of course," Grey offered, though his eyes were as steely as ever. Bryndis looked at Frida, who was biting her lip with such vigor they'd have to hit up every drugstore within a fifty mile radius and still need to scour the Internet for extra tubes of Chapstick. Then Bryndis glanced at Madge: her gawky frame, stringy grey hair and jumbled frumpy attire may have all been a cover. But there was a real kindness in her eyes, something no scoundrel could conjure. And besides, Madge had, after all, devoted most of her life to the right side of the law. If nothing else, Bryndis was pretty sure Madge wouldn't let Grey and his flunkies kill her beloved Frida. Pretty sure would have to be good enough. One of Grey's henchmen beckoned them to the secret hatch—its door flipped open, awaiting them.

"Down there! Let's get going...now!" Grey commanded. The more ominous henchman, the one with a bulging jaw and a tight *Scarface* leather jacket, pulled out his gun. Bryndis ventured down the rickety rope ladder, followed by Grey.

"Oh, God. It's you!" she exclaimed when both she and Grey finally reached the bottom. It was Grey's surprisingly comforting arms that provided refuge as Bryndis fell backwards in a swoon worthy of any Austen heroine.

Chapter Twenty-one
by Owen Magruder

Bryndis and Grey had already reached the bottom and Madge was trying to descend the rope behind them. All of a sudden, Bella adroitly thrust her oversized umbrella between Madge's legs, causing her to fall down on top of the couple.

Tony, who'd been hiding in the secret room, quickly kicked Grey's handgun across the floor to Holt, whose presence accounted for Bryndis's exclamation before she fainted. Just as quickly, Holt pointed the pistol at Grey's head and quietly said, "Freeze!" The shaken and disoriented leader of the gang slowly arose with his hands stretched high above his head.

Madge, meanwhile, had appeared to had struck her head heavily on the floor as she fell down the rope ladder. Grey's two cohorts in crime—seeing what was happening below—quickly vacated The Neglected Word through the back door and into the arms of Detective Morris Krill and two of his officers.

Frida screamed, "Auntie Bryn! Auntie Bryn!" as she dashed down the rope ladder to her aunt's side. The wail of the Harpshead's volunteer ambulance muffled Frida's sobbing as she embraced her aunt's limp body.

Two state police cruisers and a van arrived with the ambulance, and Madge, Grey and their two accomplices were bundled off to the local jail to await transfer to a state facility to be charged with multiple crimes, including kidnapping and firearms possession. Tony accompanied Grey, his paramour Madge, and their thugs, while Frida and Holt went with Bryndis in the ambulance to the local Community Hospital.

Bryndis was kept in the ER long enough to ascertain that she had not suffered a major injury in her fall and was released to go back to her small apartment with Frida and Holt. And just to be sure it was the real Holt, Bryn checked his back for any tattoos.

Once there, Aunt Snaedis fixed them a delicious dinner as they sat around the small dining table in silence trying to comprehend what had happened to them during the past few days. Tony joined them for dessert.

* * * * *

Meanwhile, Rambler, being no fool, had fired up his VW van and headed southwest as fast as his ancient transportation and the legal speed limits would allow. It was not until he'd crossed the Oklahoma border that he started to relax. *Man, I don't want any more of this nonsense. Code Books, Bibles, people with guns. Life's too short for this, man! I don't need this,* he thought as he'd driven Interstate 44 towards Chandler.

It had been dark for more than three hours when he finally pulled into a ramshackle campground in the middle of Lincoln County, hooked up his wheeled home and set out his charcoal burner to fix a late supper. The canned beef stew raised his depressed spirits as he savored the hot Oklahoma air.

He took out the white package that had already caused him so much grief. He contemplated it with much ambivalence. Supposedly this book, that so many people were willing to kill for, was the key to vast riches, the likes of which he, certainly, would never see in his lifetime. *Man, what's the big deal about a pile of gold?* he thought. *You can't eat it and you sure as hell can't smoke it!* He took a long drag on his after-dinner joint. *Why do people get so uptight over a little—hell, a lot—of gold shiny metal? Look at me! I don't need lots of gilt. Got my home on wheels, my freedom, no cares— now that I'm away from all of those crazies.*

Now what am I going to do with you? You white rectangular bundle of trouble. Rambler looked down at the code book beside his grill. *Maybe I should just burn you and save me and a lot of other people—nice people—a peck of trouble.* He started to put the package on the grill, but his conscience grabbed him. *Hadn't Holt sent me to Mexico to get the code book for him? Hadn't Holt paid all my expenses?*

Maybe I should just put it in a box and mail it back to him. I just don't know. I just don't know. . . .

* * * * *

Back in Harpshead, Aunt Snaedis had finished clearing the dessert plates when Bryndis fixed Holt and Tony with her blue-gray eyes. "Now tell us what this is all about. This Bible. These horrid people. Tell us, please, what has been going on?"

Holt lowered his eyes and slowly began, "All right. Here's how it all started. . . ."

Chapter Twenty-two
by Leslie Matthews Stansfield

"Well, it kinda started in Mexico," Holt began.

"Wait," Bryndis interrupted. "I gotta know. Are Madge and Bella for real?"

Tony burst out laughing. "Good gracious, no! Those two are about as deep undercover as it gets. They are completely unorthodox and brilliant. They come across as two bumbling old dolts, but it's all an act. They're retired and have no families." He stopped and blew out a long breath. He looked at his audience and shook his head. "They've been at this for years. They make it look easy. They'll probably come here later. You'll see. I mean Madge as Grey's lover? Never! It was all a ruse on her part to infiltrate Grey's gang. Madge won't stay in jail."

The group sat in silence for a bit. Bryndis tried to picture those women as intelligent. *It must take a Mensa IQ to continually act that stupid,* she mused.

"Well," Frida said, "I want to know the whole story. Ever since I got here, I couldn't decide if this was a mystery or a very bad comedy! The whole thing with Madge being with Mr. Grey had me in quite a quandary." She paused, proud of her use of the word *quandary*. "Madge and Bella rescued me, hid me and called Aunt Bryn. They had plenty of chances to turn me over to Mr. Grey. They could've killed me themselves. I just couldn't believe that Madge was in cahoots with Mr. Grey. I was feeling like I was going crazy."

Tony nudged her shoulder. "I don't blame you, kiddo. The last few days had me questioning my own sanity too, and I've been in it from the beginning. Bella and Madge were in it from the start. They infiltrated an artifacts smuggling ring just after nine-eleven. The thinking of the government was that if we bombed Iraq—which we did—artifacts and other stolen valuables would be smuggled out and sold on the black market. They've been at it ever since."

"What does this have to do with Holt's Bible?" Bryndis asked. "That didn't come from the Middle East."

"No, it didn't. Where it came from is another story. However, when my brother wound up with the Bible, the group I work for began to hear talk about smugglers looking for it. At first, I had no idea it was the Bible that Holt had told me about. Once I figured it out, I knew that Holt was in danger as well anyone associated with him."

"Why couldn't you just tell him?" Frida asked.

Tony looked at his brother sheepishly, cleared his throat and said, "Well, Holt was going through a rather tough time and I wasn't sure he could be trusted."

Holt bowed his head and said, "I was getting to like Rambler's lifestyle. I just wanted to let it all go."

"Who's Rambler?" Frida asked.

Aunt Snaedis held up her hand. "Stop. Just tell us the basics. There are so many twists and turns that we could be here all night."

"I don't care!" shouted Frida. "I want every little detail."

"Okay, okay," Tony said. "Holt came home from Mexico and told me that weird story about the Bible. I didn't think anything of it. But, a few weeks later, word began to circulate within the artifacts smuggling ring that a Bible they were tracking was lost. Madge said that Grey was going crazy looking for it. He suddenly took some of his guys and went to Mexico." Tony stood and stretched.

"Keep going," Frida urged.

"Okay, so when I heard them say 'Mexico' I thought about Holt. I tried to ask him about it." Tony gave Holt a glare. "But he said he'd sold it."

"Holt, why would you do that?" Bryndis asked. "You obviously didn't sell it."

"Because I didn't want my brother poking into my business," Holt said testily. "I don't trust many people."

"Speaking of people," Bryndis said, "how could *I* not know Holt had a twin brother?"

"Sad story," Holt interjected. "Remember, my family moved here when we were in seventh grade. Well, there was a reason we moved here. My brother— my twin brother, that is—had tried to kill me. He was diagnosed as having a severe personality disorder. He was truly a borderline psychopath. My aunt and uncle took him in. My uncle was a psychiatrist. So we moved to Harpshead. My mother was heartbroken. It was really weird for us to pretend like he didn't really exist."

"How horrible for you," Aunt Snaedis cried.

"How did he wind up with Mr. Grey's gang?" Frida asked.

"Well," said Tony, "first of all, once he—Vince— turned eighteen, he was free to look for us. He didn't because by then he was on his way to making his name as a hit man. I came across him a few years ago when I was undercover. Who ever thinks his brother will grow up to be a killer for hire? Long story short, the FBI began to suspect Vince of killing a few people, but they couldn't prove it. I was the link. When he showed up working for Mr. Grey, Madge and Bella began watching him. We're pretty sure he killed the contact we were to meet at The Book Lovers' Convention."

Bryndis almost choked on her coffee. "Booth 153? Remember that note I found in Holt's room, Tony?"

Tony stared at Holt. "Yeah, I do. Holt, how did you know about Booth 153?"

"How does that pertain to this?" Holt asked.

"Booth 153 was the location of a book smuggler," said Tony. "We heard he was onto the Bible."

"I saw something about a rare book dealer looking for Bibles," Holt said. "It was on a book collectors' chat room on the internet. I was going to take the Bible to him at his booth—153—at the book convention."

"Okay, so who's Rambler?" Frida interjected.

Bryndis noticed her niece's eyes were wide with expectation. *Frida is really enjoying this*, she thought. *She'll probably want to join the FBI after this.*

"I met Rambler when I started going camping last year," explained Holt. "I know he's a little different, but I really like him. He's so laid back. Anyway, once Tony asked me about the Bible, I started doing some digging of my own. I started reading on the internet about a Bible with a code book. All sorts of crazy stuff! There was a rumor that Davey Crockett and some of his friends originally created the code book to hide the directions to some Aztec gold they'd found. Some rumors say the code book—or codex—was part of Crockett's genealogy and some say it's hidden somewhere else. Some say it's in his Bible. But all of the rumors say that to find the gold you need both the Bible and the code. When Crockett was killed in the Alamo, someone smuggled the Bible to Mexico. Some say it was the Mexican General Santa Anna or one of his aides. After that, there's no mention of it until recently. Anyway, Rambler loves to go to Mexico. I asked him to look around and not tell anyone but me if he found something."

"So, he found the code book?" Aunt Snaedis asked.

"I have no idea," Holt said. "Before he could show me what he'd found, Grey showed up at my door and grabbed me."

"Okay," Aunt Snaedis said, "how did Mr. Grey even know to look for Holt?"

"We think Grey's guys tracked him through his hotel in Mexico," Tony explained. "Remember, Holt didn't know what he had in that Bible or that others were searching for it. There was no reason for him to hide."

"And now here we sit," Aunt Snaedis said pensively. "No further along than before."

Frida yawned and the group decided they all needed their rest. They agreed to disband until the next day.

* * * * *

The banging of trash cans caused Bryndis to startle awake. She wanted to return to her dream. She couldn't quite grasp it. The dream flickered about in her brain, an elusive phantom teasing her. Images of the past few days danced around: Holt's apartment; Bella and Madge; the box of candy; and headlights in her rear view mirror. All of them swirled together and mixed with a feeling of fear—the worry that something would happen to Frida.

She sat up, put her feet in her slippers then took her robe from the bed post. She hoped that making coffee would help. She quietly exited her bedroom, careful not to wake Frida who was sleeping on a blow-up mattress on the floor.

A few minutes later, with a cup of dark roast coffee in hand, she stood looking out her window, staring at nothing in particular. She kept trying to grab on to the indefinable image that was poking around in her brain.

Her cell phone beeped, telling her there was a message. It was from Tony. *Hey, Bryn, are you opening the book shop today?*

Bryndis texted back, *I wasn't planning on it. I might change my mind. Still waking up. Made coffee. Want some?*

"Good morning," said Frida, startling Bryndis. Frida was already dressed and ready for the day.

"Frida Bonita, you just scared the heck out of me! I didn't hear you get up. Tony's probably coming over. I'm going to throw some clothes on."

"Okay. Auntie Bryn?"

"Yes?"

"I can't stop thinking about the last few days. My gut says that we're missing something. My head says my gut is wrong."

Bryndis chuckled. "I know, sweetie. I feel the same way. I think it's because so much has happened in such a short period of time. And still we don't know what's at the bottom of it all."

Bryndis jogged into her bedroom and grabbed her jeans and a clean top. She dressed and brushed her hair. As she was walking out into the kitchen, there was a knock at the door. Although she assumed it was Tony, the last few days of dangerous people shoving their way through doors had left her a little nervous about answering the door.

"Hey, it's Tony. I need coffee bad."

Bryn smiled and answered the door. "I have just the thing," she said, smiling at him. She was so grateful that the nightmare was over and Frida and Holt were safe.

She poured Tony a cup of coffee. "What's on your agenda for today?" she asked.

"Nothing exciting. I'm truly glad to be able to say that. Are you sure you don't want to open the shop? Wouldn't getting back into a routine calm your nerves?"

Before she could answer, there was a frantic banging on her door. Afraid it was Holt or Aunt Snaedis in trouble, Bryndis ran over and yanked it open. Bella and Madge tumbled in. Both women were red-faced and out of breath.

"Oh, thank goodness you're okay! We were scared to death," Bella said.

"Why?" asked Bryndis. "Grey and his gang are in jail."

"Well, we have a bigger problem now," Madge said. "Yellow Jacket was found murdered in the parking garage below the convention center. Since Mr. Grey and his companions were already in custody when he was killed, they're in the clear. Something else is going on!"

"Who's Yellow Jacket?" Frida asked.

"That crazy guy who we talked to at The Book Lovers' Convention," said Madge.

"You *knew* him?" Bryndis and Frida said in chorus.

"Yes, yes, he was one of our informants at the convention." Madge waved her hand at them, indicating she had more important issues on her mind.

"How can he be dead?" cried Tony. "I talked to him a few hours ago."

"It happened and now we deal with it. You're to go to the morgue in St. Louis, Tony. We thought all this was about the Bible. But something else is going on," said Madge.

Tony gazed at Bryndis and Frida. "Are they safe?" he asked the two elderly women. "Oh no! Holt! What about my brother?"

"Relax, another officer's here with us. He's with Holt now downstairs. We think Bryndis and Frida are safe. But, an officer's coming to stay with them too," Madge said.

"Can't you do it?" Tony asked. "I'd feel so much better if all three of them were with you."

"We're supposed to go back to the convention to help search for Yellow Jacket's killer. We'll stay here until backup arrives, though," Madge promised.

"Why can't we all go to the convention?" Frida asked. "Aunt Bryn has tickets. We were already there anyway."

"Are you out of your mind, Frida?" Bryndis choked. "Give it a rest, Nancy Drew."

"Honey, you're safer here. We can't put you in any more danger," Bella said, patting Frida's hand that rested on the table.

"Well, I can't sit here all day," Bryndis said. "Can I open my shop at least?" Bryndis wrapped her arms around herself. Suddenly, she felt chilled to the bone.

"I think that's the best idea," Tony answered. "It will be harder for anyone to get to you if you're in public. What do you think, ladies?" he asked Madge and Bella.

"We'll make some phone calls," replied Madge. "Tony, you get going. We'll figure the rest out."

Tony grabbed his jacket and went over to Bryndis. He gave her a quick hug. "Be safe," he whispered in her ear.

They all came down the stairs from the apartments and around the complex onto the front sidewalk. "You have a very short commute," Madge said, smiling.

"A lot has happened since the last time I was here," Holt said, coming towards them. "It seems like a life time ago."

"That it does," Bryndis agreed.

The six of them stood in silence for a moment, just staring at The Neglected Word, each with their own thoughts. "Okay, here we—"

Bryndis was interrupted by a honking horn. She couldn't believe her eyes. The wackiest 1960's Volkswagen bus careened into a parking space across the street. Rambler scrambled out. *Oh, of course, who else could possibly own that van?* Bryndis thought.

"Holt, man! I thought you were dead!" Rambler stopped just long enough to look both ways and ran over to them. He and Holt embraced each other and thumped each other on the back.

"I thought I was gonna be!" Holt said.

"Yo, little lady!" Rambler said to Bryndis. "It's good to see you. Last time I saw you, you were lookin' for my buddy here."

"Hello," Madge said. "Who might you be?"

"Oh, sorry, this is Rambler, a friend of mine," Holt said. "Rambler, these people are looking into that issue with the Bible from Mexico."

"Cool," Rambler replied.

Because Holt hadn't volunteered anything to the group about Rambler finding the code book, Bryndis kept her mouth shut too. She unlocked the door to her store.

"Don't open the door!" Bella barked, trotting over to Bryndis. She pushed Bryndis to the side. She drew a gun from a holster concealed by her jacket, reached out and grasped the door handle. She looked carefully around the frame of the door, then opened the door a tiny crack and listened. Again, she studied the door frame. Bella carefully eased in the door as Madge went in behind her. Together they checked every inch of the store.

"Wow, man! Heavy stuff. You *are* in real danger! They should bring in a bomb-sniffing dog," Rambler said. "Why don't you come hang out with me? We can travel around in the van. They'll never figure out where you are. Heck, *we* probably won't know where we are."

Holt chuckled. "You're probably right about that. Honestly, buddy, I need to lay off the weed for a bit."

Rambler nodded. "That's cool, man. That's cool. But all you folks seem major tense. You might want to wait until tomorrow to cut back."

Madge appeared in the door way. "All clear. C'mon in."

Bryndis was glad for Frida's sake that the discussion about weed was temporarily tabled. Although, Rambler did have a point about their stress level.

Stepping through the door, Bryndis inhaled deeply. The smell of cinnamon and coffee still hung faintly in the air. The aroma brought her a sense of peace. *Who needs weed when you've got cinnamon and coffee?* Bryn thought.

"Frida Bonita, why don't you go pick yourself out a book? You can sprawl out in the beanbag chair."

"Okay. I think I'll just re-read *Jane Eyre*, but I'll look around first."

Bryndis was amused to see Rambler making his way around the store. He seemed to be soaking it all in. She and Holt looked at each other and smiled. Rambler looked nothing less than enthralled.

"Roberts, would you call in and tell them what's going on and see when someone is coming to relieve us?" Madge asked one of the officers.

"Sure thing, Madge," Officer Roberts replied. He took out his phone, punched a few buttons and put it to his ear.

"Well, I guess I'll go into my office and get things settled," Bryndis said. She called out to Frida, "Any possibilities?" She was hoping Frida might find something that would suit her fancy. The girl had read *Jane Eyre* at least five times that Bryndis was aware of.

"Maybe," Frida responded. "I'm not sure yet." Bryndis was about to go see what books Frida had labeled "possibilities" when she saw Rambler eyeing the coffee machine.

"Rambler, can I make you some coffee?" Bryndis asked.

"Absolutely not!" cried Rambler, shoving her backwards. "Do *not* touch that machine! We all need to get out of here, NOW! There's a bomb in that machine."

Bella and Madge were next to Rambler in a flash. He said something in a tone too quiet for Bryndis to hear and pointed at the upper part of the machine.

"Everyone get out!" Bella yelled.

Bryndis was frozen in place. It was as if all the air was sucked out of the room. She felt like she was looking at a movie screen as Holt ran for Frida, steering her out the door. Officer Roberts was right next to him. Rambler was jogging right behind Madge. Bryndis caught a slight whiff of weed as he went by. She was jolted by Bella who grabbed her arm and hustled her out the door.

"Go to your aunt's shop!" Madge yelled.

Holt grabbed Frida's arm and they began heading to Aunt Snaedis's shop. Surprisingly, Rambler, who Bryndis thought would be right on Holt's heels, got behind the group like a sheep dog, urging them all toward the store. Bryndis turned to see Bella take a step to the side, then fall in behind him. Her phone was in her hand and she was barking orders at someone on the other end.

"What in the world?" Aunt Snaedis asked, as she was almost trampled by the group as they rushed into her store.

Madge grabbed the *open* sign on the door and flipped it to *closed.* "Lock it!" she snapped at Aunt Snaedis. Aunt Snaedis grabbed the keys from around her neck and immediately did as she was told, then she closed the blinds on the windows.

"Everyone get in the office," Bella said, "and stay there. The bomb squad is on the way."

"Bomb squad?" asked Aunt Snaedis.

Frida, Holt and Rambler all began talking at once. Bryndis caught snippets of their words.

"Reaching for a book—" said Frida.

"Saw a wire that didn't belong—" Rambler was saying.

"Next thing I knew—" Holt said.

Bryndis wasn't really listening. She was thinking about the unopened box of candy left on her doorstep with the strange odor—and now a bomb in her coffee pot. Someone was trying to kill her.

* * * * *

It was Aunt Snaedis who realized Bryndis was in shock. "Oh, my good Lord!" she exclaimed. "Honey, come sit down; you look positively awful."

Holt and Officer Roberts almost bumped into each other as they both raced to get a chair for her. Roberts deferred to Holt. Holt grabbed a chair from the wall where the dressing rooms were. He jogged back with it and held Bryndis's arm to keep her from falling as she practically collapsed into it.

"Auntie Bryn, you're shaking," Frida said.

Bryndis wanted to be strong for Frida. She didn't want Frida to know there was anything wrong, but fear overwhelmed her like Niagara Falls would a mouse.

Madge grabbed another chair from the wall and plunked it down in front of Bryndis. Sitting in front of her, Madge said, "Close your eyes and take deep breaths."

"The candy," Bryndis mumbled. "Remember the box of candy?"

"What candy?" Holt asked.

"There was a box of candy left outside my shop door the day we found you missing, Holt," Bryndis croaked out. "I think it was poisoned. And now this bomb. Someone is trying to kill me."

"And that someone cannot possibly be Grey and his cronies," Madge said.

The sound of the sirens racing through town became louder as they closed in on Bryndis's shop. "Sounds like the bomb squad has arrived," Bella said.

Madge nodded toward the door as an indication to Officer Roberts to go work with the team. Aunt Snaedis unlocked the door to let him out. Bella went with him.

"Bryndis, do you still have the box of candy?" asked Madge.

"No, I threw it in the trash and I guess Aunt Snaedis put it out in the dumpster," said Bryndis.

"Oh, dear!" added Snaedis, "I did just that and the garbage men collected the trash last night."

"Oh, no," moaned Bryndis.

"All right," said Madge, trying to get Bryndis to focus, "I want you to think about that box of candy. When did you notice it?"

Bryndis related the story of Tony finding the box and bringing it in the shop. She told her about opening it later, the unusual odor and tossing it back in the trash.

"Madge!" cried Bryndis, "that candy smelled like bitter almonds. I think someone injected poison in those candies."

"You may be right, dear," agreed Madge, "but without anything to send to the lab, it's a moot point."

At this point, Bella returned and knocked on the door. Snaedis let her in and Bella said, "Definitely a bomb. The bomb squad isn't sure if turning the coffee maker on will set the bomb off or not. They want to unplug it and take it into the truck."

"How do they know there isn't a timer on it?" Holt asked.

"They have devices that listen for sounds like gears and ticking," explained Bella. "There doesn't appear to be a timing mechanism. If that were the case, my guess is that the bomb would have gone off when Bryndis attempted to add water to make the coffee."

Through the blinds, it was possible to see people stopping and trying to look through the windows, obviously wondering why the shop was closed. Bryndis realized that Aunt Snaedis was losing customers. The shop was her sole income.

"Can't my aunt open her store?" Bryndis asked. "It's not fair for her to lose business. People are all standing around and gawking out front. I'm sure someone will want to buy the perfect dress to wear to a bombing," she said, smiling.

Madge laughed and patted Bryndis's knee. "Okay, you're feeling better. You're even succumbing to the bizarre humor people develop under stress."

"If you don't laugh, you'll cry," added Holt.

"Exactly!" Bella and Madge said in unison.

"What about this?" Frida asked, showing them a scarf with an Angry Birds theme—bombs and all— which she pulled from a counter. "You could pair it with this," she said, donning a hat with an orange and yellow flame on it.

"Hey, good call. The bomb squad needs you as their fashion consultant," Bella said, laughing.

Bryndis moved the chairs back to their original position and sat quietly watching the action around her.

She was too emotionally exhausted to move. Holt and Rambler left with Bella to get coffee for everyone. Aunt Snaedis drew up the blinds and unlocked the door. Customers began to drift into the store. Frida jumped right in, helping a few young girls look for clothes. Bryndis watched Madge wander slowly around the store, her shrewd eyes following everyone and each move they made.

Suddenly, there was a muffled *throooom*. Madge walked over to the door and looked out. "Bomb's detonated safely," she said. Bryndis and everyone in the shop, with the exception of Aunt Snaedis, joined Madge on the walk outside the store. Men and women in white suits with blue patches reading "Bomb Squad" continued to walk around.

"Hey, look! They really brought a dog," Rambler said in an awed voice. "Way cool."

In her peripheral vision, Bryndis caught Madge doing an eye-roll. Bryndis brought her hand up to her mouth so no one would see her grin. She had to admit that Rambler was growing on her. There was something about Rambler that Bryndis found endearing. She thought about him getting behind the group, herding them toward Aunt Snaedis's store. He was certainly loyal to Holt. There was simultaneously both a gentleness and strength about him. Although laid back, Bryndis sensed he was also as wily as a fox.

Officer Roberts strolled over and wiggled his finger in a "come here" motion to Bella and Madge. The threesome huddled and quietly conferred. Taking a moment to look around, Bryndis also noticed Holt and Rambler now had their backs to the group and were whispering to each other. She wondered what that was about, but eventually Rambler and Holt went over to speak to the detectives. Finally, the detectives moved further outside with Holt and Rambler. Bryndis saw

Frida watching all of this clandestine activity. Frida turned toward Bryndis and frowned.

"Okay," Bella said, breaking Bryndis away from her own thoughts. "We're all going down to the station to go over the events of this case from the beginning. There's something we're missing, and we have to figure it out, now!"

"And Rambler's coming with us," said Holt, returning with his friend. "He's involved in this too."

Bryndis saw Madge's eyes narrow. She looked angry. Still, Madge said nothing. Then, without another word, everyone got into three different squad cars. Officer Roberts helped her and Frida into his squad car. Bella and Madge went with Holt and Rambler. Bryndis couldn't imagine what Rambler and the code book had to do with any of this, but she sure hoped it would help answer the question of who was trying to kill her.

* * * * *

At the station, Bryndis was hungry and had a headache the size of Texas. She wondered how many ways Bella and Madge could ask questions about the events that had led them here. Frida Bonita was still perky and soaking it all in. She looked like a puppy watching people throw a ball around. Outwardly, she kept her Jane Eyre calm, but her eyes betrayed her fascination. Holt and Rambler looked as exhausted as Bryndis felt.

Detective Krill came in finally and asked to talk to Bella and Madge. Behind him was a man in a suit. Bryndis didn't recognize him. The two women joined the detectives outside the room and after a few minutes of whispering, nodding, and shaking heads, the suited man came back in.

"My name is Inspector Charles Miller. I'm with the FBI," the man explained. "We have our antiquities people examining both the Bible that Ms. Palmer supplied us and the code book that we just received from Mr.—um—Rambler. I have no idea if they'll be able to crack the code now that we have both the Bible and the codex, but they'll try. Hopefully, it will explain *some* of what's been going on. What's more urgent are the multiple attempts on Ms. Palmer's life. She had no more access to the two items in question than Mr. Furst or Mr. Rambler, so we're uncertain why she seems to have been targeted."

"I'd like to know that myself, but can I have a sandwich first?" Bryndis asked. "I'm starving."

"Ditto," Holt added.

"I'll order food," Bella said, looking at her cell phone. "It's three o'clock. You folks have been a great help. Let's hope Inspector Miller here can give us some answers."

As the group consumed fast food, they had questions for each other.

"Well, I'm lost," Holt said.

"No kidding," Bryndis said. "I wonder how Tony is making out at the morgue. I don't know if he even knows what's going on."

"He probably called in and someone told him. We can ask Bella and Madge," Holt said.

"I think we should just take off in the van," Rambler said. "It's safer and less confusing."

Bryndis shuddered to think what her sister would do if Bryndis took Frida cross country in the weed mobile.

Eventually, Krill and Miller came back in and sat down at the table with them and they reviewed the facts as they knew them so far.

"Honestly," Miller said. "We're still somewhat in the dark—"

"Does The Book Lovers' Convention have anything to do with it?" Frida asked.

"Yes, but we're not sure what," he replied. "The convention is still in full swing, and, of course, with the murder of Yellow Jacket there, the killer or killers may not know that we've captured Grey and his men, and we have a chance of catching whoever it is if we act fast."

"We have a plan," Bella said. "It might answer our questions, particularly the one that involves who's targeting Bryndis. However, in order for the plan to work, we need all of your help," she explained.

"I'm going on record," Madge said, "as being opposed to this. I think it's too dangerous, but I agreed to let you all hear it and make your own decisions."

Frida, it appeared, had already decided to go along with whatever the plan was.

* * * * *

"Bryn! Holt!" Tony exclaimed as he saw his brother and the others entering the exhibition hall at The Book Lovers' Convention. "What are you all doing here?"

"Frida wanted to actually visit the convention before she has to leave," replied Bryndis. "And they wouldn't let me open my shop, so..."

"Why couldn't she open the shop?" Tony asked. "Grey is locked up."

"*Was* locked up," Bella said. "He made bail. He got out an hour ago."

"Bail? How could he possibly make bail? What about the others?" asked Tony.

"They're still behind bars, for now. However, now that Grey's out, it's only a matter of time," Bella said. "How's your investigation going into Yellow Jacket's murder?"

"Slow, I'm afraid. We processed the crime scene and sent everything in to the lab. Whoever it was wiped everything clean. No finger prints. I'm hoping the lab can find something."

"Too bad," said Madge.

"Well, I need to be getting back," Tony said. "I'm glad I caught you for a bit. I'm so relieved you're okay." He hugged Bryndis. To Bella and Madge, he added, "I'm counting on you to take good care of them." He looked around. "Where's Officer Roberts?"

"We let him stay behind. Grey won't show up here."

"Are you all sharing a room?" Tony asked, again eyeing Holt.

"No, silly," Bryndis said. "Frida and I share a room, Bella and Madge are across the hall, and Holt's room adjoins theirs. It's like our own little safety compound."

"Okay, I guess you're in good hands. Let me know if you need me. After I get back, I'll be at the station for a while." With a wave, he was off.

Bryndis watched Tony walk across the hall and out the door. Turning to Madge, she said, "Did you see anyone follow him? Do you think he believed us?"

Madge looked around and said, "Well, it really doesn't matter what he believed, but yes, I think he believed us. I didn't see anyone follow him. If someone was watching him here, they saw you come in."

"What if the person knows about the bomb squad and knows we lied?" Frida asked.

"Then they're aware we aren't sure if Tony is still being watched. We've protected him by keeping him out of the loop. He'll understand," Madge said.

"He's definitely annoyed that I'm here," Holt added. "I don't blame him. I'd feel the same in his shoes."

"He'll understand later. Besides, he trusts me," Bryndis added.

"Of course he trusts *you*," Holt said. "It's me he's worried about. I wish we could have told him that Roberts is here and staying with me."

"The less he knows, the better," Bella reminded them.

"Can we look around now?" Frida asked. "I really want to make the most of the time we have."

"Of course, we can," Bella said. "You lead, we'll follow."

* * * * *

It was almost eleven o'clock that night by the time Frida began to wind down. Bryndis sensed the others were as exhausted as she was. Frida, thankfully, had enough energy for all of them. All of the adults enjoyed spoiling her. Madge and Bella bought her a Book Lovers' Convention jacket, backpack, pajama set and a water bottle. Holt bought her a number of Playaway audio books, and Bryndis antied up for a number of Sherlock Holmes and Agatha Christie books. Bryndis saw Detective Miller a number of times talking to different vendors. It was harder than she thought to act like she'd never seen him before. She hoped he was able to get the information he needed and that he found whoever had killed the yellow-suited vendor known as Yellow Jacket. She wondered if Miller had seen anyone following them.

As they dragged themselves to their rooms, Bryndis was thrilled to see Frida yawn. All Bryndis wanted to do was collapse into bed. She was worried Frida would have her up all night chatting about things. Bryndis was desperately hoping Frida would not get a second wind. When they reached their hotel rooms, Bryndis gave Madge and Bella an extra key to her room.

"Remember," Madge cautioned. "Don't open that door for anyone. Bella, Roberts and I all have radios to keep in touch with Inspector Miller. If anyone knocks on your door, just push the number *one* on the cell I gave you. It'll connect you right to me. Once you're inside, put the chain across the door and lock it."

"I thought you said we'd be safe here," Bryndis said. "You said Mr. Grey wouldn't come here."

"I did say that, and I believe it's true. However, I'm not taking any chances. If you do as I ask, everything will be super safe," Madge said.

"Okay, okay," Bryndis huffed. All the extra warnings and precautions were making her nervous.

When Bryndis closed the door to their room, Frida said, "I'm going to wear my new pajamas tonight. Is that okay?"

The thought of wearing something straight out of a bag without washing it first gave Bryndis the heebie-jeebies, but she didn't want to dampen Frida's fun. "Well, okay. I think your mom might want you to wash them first, but it's your call," she said diplomatically, sliding the chain on the door.

"Great," Frida said. "We can wash them before I go home. What Mom doesn't know won't hurt her."

Bryndis smiled. "I'm going to take a shower. Do you need anything first?"

"Nope. I can't wait to try one of the Sherlock Holmes books. I like to see if I can guess the ending. Usually can't, but it's fun to try."

Going into the bathroom, Bryndis was thrilled to see the Jacuzzi tub. The attached shower fixture also had a massaging head, but Bryn wanted to sit and soak. The perfectly white towels stored beneath the sink on a shelf with a glass door looked seductively soft. She opened the door and took one out. She moaned slightly as she hugged it against herself. This was exactly what she needed.

About forty minutes later, dressed in her super cozy sweats, Bryndis exited the bathroom and saw Frida sound asleep on top of the covers with a book open on her chest. The Sherlock Holmes book was the crowning touch to the tableau. Bryn couldn't think of a better way to fall asleep.

As Bryndis sat on the side of her bed, she heard a commotion from across the street. She went and looked out the window.

"What's all the screaming?" Frida asked, sitting up.

"I dunno. Something is going on across the street."

There was a knock on the door. "It's Bella. Quick let me in."

Frida ran over, undid the chain and opened the door. She stepped back so Bella could enter.

"They believe we've trapped the person or people who killed Yellow Jacket. We're going down to serve as backup. Do not, under any circumstances, leave this room. If something happens, like the fire alarm goes off, look through the peephole and don't open the door until you see Officer Roberts. Got it?"

Bryndis and Frida nodded.

Bella left, closing the door behind her. As she slid the chain across the door, Frida asked, "Why would she think the fire alarm would go off?"

"In times of emergencies, some crazy people just pull the fire alarm," Bryndis said. "With so many people running around screaming, there's no telling what someone will do."

"Oh," was all Frida said.

It's also a good way to get people to leave their rooms, Bryndis thought.

* * * * *

Five minutes later, the sound of police sirens disturbed the night. Frida put on her new coat. "I think I'd like to be prepared," she said.

"Good thinking," Bryndis said. "I hope it's all for nothing, but I'm going to put my coat on, too."

As the two of them stood quietly looking out the window down at the commotion, Frida turned to Bryndis and smiled. "I guess this is what my mom means when she talks about being all dressed-up with no place to go."

Bryndis laughed. "Yes, this is a perfect example of that."

That was the exact moment the fire alarm went off. Frida's eyes widened and a shiver of fear shot down Bryndis's spine. Bryndis ran to the door and looked through the peephole. She watched as the door across from them opened and Roberts stepped out. Bryndis opened her door and said to Frida, "Do not let go of my hand."

The other guests were all heading toward the exit to the stairs. When there was no one left in the hall, Roberts told Holt to head to the exit at the end of the hallway, and Bryndis and Frida to follow. They were almost to the exit when the door to their right flew open. Bryndis and Frida screamed as a man in a black ski mask tackled Roberts, took his gun, pushed him to the ground and hit him with a gun handle, knocking him out. The door on the left burst open and two more men in black ski masks rushed at Holt. One of the men knocked Holt unconscious. Two of the masked men dragged Holt and Roberts into the room on the left while the third waved his gun indicating that Bryndis and Frida should follow them inside.

Bryndis and Frida huddled together in a corner of the room while Holt and Roberts were bound and gagged with duct tape. Bryndis's mind was racing. How could these men possibly have known where she was? It was clear the men were prepared and waiting for them. Were Bella and Madge on Mr. Grey's side after all? It had to be that. Nothing else made sense. They were the only ones who knew.

"Let Frida go!" she cried. "I don't care what you do to me, but let her go. She's just a girl. She hasn't seen your faces. Please let her go."

One of the men reached up and yanked off his ski mask. She didn't recognize him. He was tall, husky and had salt and pepper hair. He took off his black coat, revealing a bus boy's jacket. It was rumpled, but she doubted anyone would notice that. He pulled on the lapel of the jacket and stepped in front of the mirror.

Frida's arms tightened around Bryndis's waist. Bryndis knew they were on their own. No help was coming. Even the cell phone she had was probably useless.

"Let's get them to the freight elevator," the man said. He walked to the closet and took out two long, black, garment bags.

The other two men grabbed Bryndis and Frida and yanked them forward. One of the men stepped behind them and put his gun against Bryndis's back. "One sound and you're both dead," he whispered.

"Weston Blake," Bryndis said calmly.

The man yanked off his mask. "Very good," he said.

The third man reached up and removed his mask. Bryndis gasped. It was Tony. "Say goodnight," he said as he covered her mouth with a cloth.

* * * * *

Bryndis's head was spinning. Her thoughts were jumbled. As she began to wake, she realized she was hot and having trouble breathing. She could barely move her arms. It began to come back to her. She must be in one of the garment bags. She slowly worked her arm across her body and upward. By her forehead she found the back part of the zipper. She dug at it until she got one of her fingers out. Then she moved the zipper down to her stomach. This allowed her to get her arms out and then her upper body.

Sitting up and taking deep breaths, she realized she must be in the back of a truck. The truck bed seemed to be square. Her eyes were now adjusting to the darkness. There was another bag right beside her. Bryndis rolled to her side and unzipped it. Frida was inside. She was unconscious. Bryndis leaned her face over Frida's. She could feel the young girl's soft, shallow breaths. *Thank God she's breathing!*

Bryndis kicked her feet and wiggled out of the bag. She crawled to the door of the van and yanked at the handle. It was obviously locked on the outside. She thought of banging, but was afraid that would make things worse. She looked around, hoping to find a weapon. If she couldn't find that, maybe she could think of a way to break the lock. She scooted over to the wall of the truck and began to feel around.

After a few minutes, she'd only found a few bits of rope. She was beginning to lose hope when she heard it. Sirens! She felt the truck speed up. It swayed a bit. She quickly crawled over to Frida. She curled up next to her and held her tightly. The truck swayed again. She prayed that God would keep them safe. They were still alive, so there was hope. The truck lurched to the right and Bryndis and Frida slid and banged into a wall. Suddenly, they were rolling, rolling, rolling! She lost her grip on Frida. Bryndis screamed. Her body slammed down like a rag doll and her last thoughts before losing consciousness were of Frida's smile.

* * * * *

So much white light. Soft, gentle voices calling her name. "Bryn, Bryn, stay with us."

"Frida? Frida?" Bryndis whispered.

"Auntie Bryn!" came a wail that cut through the daze.

Bryndis's eyes flew open. She tried to sit up, and horrendous pain ricocheted from her head to her toes. She opened her mouth to scream, but the pain was so intense that no sound would come.

Her eyes focused on Madge. "Tony," Bryndis croaked.

"Yes, we know. He was in the truck. We suspected he was involved. The box of candy steered us in his direction. If you'd opened your store only minutes before Tony arrived, we wondered, why didn't you see the candy?"

"How did you find us?"

"I had a transmitter placed in the cell phone I gave you and I put a tracker in the pocket of the jacket I bought Frida. The cell was transmitting to us the whole time. We heard everything," Bella explained.

Bryndis closed her eyes and went back to sleep.

* * * * *

Opening her eyes later, Bryndis saw Holt sitting in a chair by her bed. He jumped up when he saw her looking at him.

"Well, hello. It's about time you woke up," he said, smiling and squeezing her hand.

"How long have I been out?" Bryndis asked.

"About 16 hours."

"Frida!"

"Bryn, Frida's in better shape than you. She was unconscious and her body was more relaxed. She's banged up, but she's going to be fine. Lia's with her. Frida hasn't stopped talking since Lia got here. No, Lia is not mad. She said she hasn't seen Frida this happy in years."

"Holt, what a mess this all is!"

"I know. I got that Bible by sheer accident. It was supposed to go to this Mr. Grey. He wanted Tony to get it from me, but I'd given it to you. I sensed someone was following me. I thought I was being paranoid, but I wanted to be sure."

"Is that why Tony was trying to kill me?"

"No. Tony didn't even know that Grey had come after me until he saw my apartment ransacked. Tony wanted you dead because he wanted your bookstore. He was working with Blake from the Laundromat and another guy. They planned to buy the bookstore after you died. We think there's something about that hidden room in your basement that they want."

"I know what it is!" cried Bryndis. "It's the painting—or something about the painting!"

"You mean that ghastly thing with the old soldier in it?" asked Holt.

"Yes, and I don't think that's just some old soldier," she replied.

"You don't think it's valuable, do you?" Holt suggested.

"I have no idea," Bryndis said. "All I know is that room was hidden until a few days ago. I'm going to have to talk to Elena again. Possibly Weston Blake knew that there was something hidden in the bookstore that was valuable and told Tony. They needed me out of the way so they could buy my shop and look for whatever it is. Once Tony found out there was a secret room, he probably got even more anxious to get rid of me. Oh, the whole thing is just petrifying. Can I have a sip of water?"

"You know," Holt said, handing her the water. "I think Grey's gang panicked because I'm Tony's brother—or because of Vince. My twin Vince is the one who got Tony involved. Mr. Grey—or whoever he is——must have thought that *I* was part of a plan to trap them. He was probably sure I went to Mexico looking for the book."

"All this started over one book?" said Bryndis. "I guess, at least that's appropriate for an owner of a bookstore." She smiled warmly at him.

"Actually, in a way, Bryn, my getting that Bible led to saving your life. If I hadn't gone missing, Tony would have killed you that day. You might have eaten one of those poison chocolates. He needed your shop and the secret room."

Bryndis nodded. It was sinking in that Tony never really cared about her. It was just a ruse to get the shop. She closed her eyes. She was not going to let Holt see her cry over Tony.

"Holt, this must be awful for you too—you lose your twin brother *and* you find out your younger brother is a crook—all in a matter of days. I would be horrified," she said, putting her arm around his shoulder.

"I feel terrible, but actually, I'm more upset over how I behaved to you. I have to apologize. The night before all this started and I snapped at you, I was a wreck because I was sure I was being followed. I was scared. I didn't want you near me because I didn't want you to get hurt, but I handled it badly," Holt said, hanging his head.

Bryndis couldn't believe the irony. "But, Holt, you gave me the blasted Bible to hide! Didn't you think they'd eventually come looking for me?"

"I thought the people were from Mexico, for crying out loud! I didn't think they'd know anything about you."

Bryndis sighed. She was too exhausted for this. "Holt, it's all okay. Let's just finish talking about this later."

Holt nodded. "I just want you to know, I'm sorry about a lot of things." He squeezed her hand and placed a gentle kiss on her forehead.

Bryndis knew it was going to take a long time to process all this. For now, she just wanted to rest.

* * * * *

It was a few more days before they allowed Bryndis to go home. Aunt Snaedis and Frida all came to get her. Bryndis was looking forward to getting back to the bookstore and her life. There were still lots of things she needed to process, but that would all happen in time.

"Aunt Snaedis, I appreciate all you've done to keep the shop open while I was in the hospital," Bryndis said.

"Oh, don't thank me. Lia and Frida did most of the work." Lia had flown out from California immediately.

Bryn looked at her niece. "Frida, I think it's about time you got back to your life. This visit of a few days is really stretching out." She was surprised to see that Frida looked crestfallen. "I loved having you, and I'm going to miss you," she added, hoping that would make Frida feel better.

Aunt Snaedis added, "Frida has helped me at my shop too. She does have a flair for fashion." Snaedis looked over at Frida and winked.

As Aunt Snaedis pulled her car up in front of the store, Bryndis noticed a big sign that said, "Welcome back, Bryndis Palmer!" Her sister Lia was standing outside with a big smile.

"Do you need help getting up to your apartment?" Aunt Snaedis asked.

"No, not right now. I think I'd like to just sit in the shop for a bit." Bryndis looked over at Holt's gym. It was nice to see it open and filled with clients.

Frida went with Aunt Snaedis. Bryndis sat down and Lia brought her a cinnamon bun and a cup of coffee. "I'm so glad you're okay," Lia said, patting her little sister's leg.

"I thought you'd want to kill me," Bryndis confessed.

Lia shook her head. "No. I haven't seen Frida happy like this since she became a teen. She's different than most teens. She struggles to fit in. With taking care of the boys, I'm afraid I'm not always there for her."

"Lia, you're a great mom. She'll be fine. Teen years are always hard," Bryndis encouraged her sister.

"Bryn, I know this has been hard on you, but I need to ask you something," Lia said.

"Anything, Lia. You know that." Bryn was concerned. Her sister looked worried.

Lia took a deep breath. "Tom has leukemia. He's going to need blood transfusions. His mom is going to help with the boys, but I'm wondering if Frida could stay with you for a while longer."

"Oh, Lia, I'm so sorry. Of course Frida can stay, but don't you need her help?" Bryndis asked.

"She's a teenager. I know she wouldn't mind helping, but she really struggles now. I haven't told her about Tom's cancer. She's been begging me to think about letting her stay with you. I figured it might be the perfect solution."

Bryndis looked into her older sister's hazel eyes. She never imagined her sister really needing her. This was a chance to be there for Lia, as Lia had always been there for her.

"Okay, Lia. But we need to let Frida make the choice. And, she may forget about staying with me once she knows her dad is sick. And, of course, what about her school?"

"It's a deal!" Lia said, and the sisters shook on it.

* * * * *

A few days later, Bryndis stood with her arm around Frida as they watched Lia get in a cab and head off to the airport. Bryndis knew there were tears in Lia's eyes. Leaving Frida behind was hard, but probably the best for Frida.

"When will your car be back?" Frida asked Bryndis. Lia, Holt and Aunt Snaedis had gotten Bryndis's Saab towed back to Harpshead. The gas line had a tiny hole in it. The car was now at a local mechanic. It would be ready in a day or so.

"Not long, sweetie. You'll be going back home once your dad is feeling better," Bryndis said, hugging her niece. "But, first, let's go down into the secret room and check out that painting. I have a sneaky suspicion that it might be valuable—"

The woman and the girl headed back into The Neglected Word and into the back room where they quickly found the loose board and lifted it up, revealing the rope entrance to the cellar. Bryndis pulled a flashlight from her pocket and started down the ladder. Frida followed slowly.

"Auntie Bryn," she whispered, "this is scary! Who would ever want to come down here?"

"Good question, Frida," replied Bryndis, reaching the bottom. She shone the flashlight around, exposing the old desk and chair. Another few swipes of the beam revealed nothing in the small grey-painted room. The two women moved to the desk and Bryndis aimed the light at the painting on the wall.

"Who is that, Auntie?" asked Frida.

"I'm not certain," said Bryndis, "but I have a suspicion that it might be General Santa Anna."

"Who?"

"The victorious Mexican general who defeated the Texans at the Alamo," said Bryndis as she examined the painting more closely. "Here, dear, hold this flashlight for me and shine it on the painting." Frida did so as Bryndis carefully pulled the large picture up and away from the wall. As it was hanging by only one nail, the painting was easily removed. Bryndis placed it face up on the desk and Frida shone the beam down on the subject's face.

"Auntie," said Frida, "do you think this is connected in any way to that Bible and the code business?"

"I wouldn't be surprised," replied her aunt. "Let's take it upstairs where we can examine it more closely." The two then climbed back up the rope ladder. Frida held the rope steady as Bryndis climbed up first with the painting hung over her shoulder by the wire in back. Once she was upstairs, she aimed the flashlight down into the cellar so Frida could see her way up. Frida's climb back up was much quicker as she was less encumbered and—of course, much younger.

Laying the painting on a table in the back room of The Neglected Word, they examined it carefully in the full light of the store. The painting showed what appeared to be a dashing Mexican man with a long mustache, dressed in full military regalia, holding a sword. Bryndis poked at the paint and the frame but it appeared quite intact for such an old picture. Then, she turned the painting over so she could better examine the back, which was covered with a thin gauzy tan cloth, tightly nailed to the edges with tiny nails. A long wire ran from one side to the other connected at the ends by old rusted screws.

"Auntie," said Frida, "look here. Part of the cloth backing seems to be pulling loose."

"It does," agreed Bryndis. They carefully tugged on the end of the backing and gently pulled it away from the painting's back. As they slowly pulled, the painting's reverse side was revealed—a darkened piece of wood. When the cloth was finally off, they could see a light brown envelope was attached—apparently by some sort of glue—to the wood backing.

"Auntie!" exclaimed Frida, "Look!"

Breathlessly, Bryndis carefully peeled the delicate envelope from the back of the painting. It was so old that it practically crumbled in her hand. She turned it over and on the front had been handwritten the words, "For the Heirs of David Crockett."

"Oh, my!" she cried. "It can't be..."

Gently using her nail, she slid her finger under the flap of the envelope and opened it. Inside was one sheet of very old parchment which she removed and unfolded. She aimed the flashlight close to the letter and read:

> "For the heirs of David Crockett: Please use the following clues in conjunction with Mr. Crockett's family Bible to retrieve the family legacy."

Following this message was a list of Bible verses—about fifteen or so in all.

"Auntie, this must be the real code! What are you going to do?" asked Frida, eyes wide.

"I don't know, Frida Bonita," said a smiling Bryndis. "But I know one thing. I'm not going to do anything about it right now. It'll just be our little secret. Okay?"

"Of course! I love secrets, Auntie Bryn!" Frida said. "What fun!"

Bryndis burst out laughing. "Yes, what fun!" And with the memory of the recent events still fresh in her mind, Bryndis carefully folded the letter up, placed it back in the envelope, and tucked it inside her pocket.

She didn't know when or if she'd recover fully from their ordeal, but she was confident that Frida would be fine. She might actually join the FBI one day. Oh, the power of books!

THE END

ABOUT THE AUTHORS

 **Amy Beth Arkawy** is a novelist, playwright, radio host, and journalist who throughout the years has learned that "perseverance is often more important than ambition or talent." Amy became interested in writing when she was in high school, where her English teacher awakened her interest in contemporary fiction, poetry, drama, and film. When she was nineteen, she submitted her first story entitled, "At Night, When No One is Watching, the Dust Collects," which was named a finalist in the *Redbook* Young Writers' Contest. Since then, Amy has written a large body of work including: full-length plays performed at various festivals in New York and across the United States, short stories, nonfiction, novels, and radio shows. Her radio and journalist careers have allowed her to interview music icons, authors, politicians, and many others.

The Cozy Cat Press group mystery was another adventure for Amy—one she enjoyed immensely: "It was a fascinating exercise. My chapter was close to the end so the challenge was to keep the facts straight, the characters consistent and move the story to its conclusion, while still leaving room for the next author." Of course, writing a group mystery is a lot different than writing a mystery by oneself: "What made it fun and exciting was also its biggest challenge. Lack of control. It was a kick playing off other authors, but like most writers, I engulf myself in control; or more aptly the illusion of control. It's really the characters who control the darn thing. They're the ones who steer the author. But that's another story."

Here is Amy's message to readers: "A group of authors set out to write a mystery together. They all made it out alive. Now you can indulge in their killer spoils!"

Amy has been nominated for the McLaren Comedy Award and has received the Nelson Algren Fiction Prize. She's a graduate of Sarah Lawrence College, where she received her undergraduate degree. She was an MFA Fellow at the University of Massachusetts, and also received an M.S. in Mental Health Counseling degree at the Long Island University. Amy grew up in the suburbs of New York City, where she currently resides. She has also worked and lived in Massachusetts and Connecticut. She also has a website: amybetharkawy.com, where you can find the titles of all her works, some samples of her work, and links to her blogs.

 **Christian Belz** is a writer who draws inspiration from all around him. His main character, Ken Knoll, works for an architect's firm that is based on an office where Christian worked in the '90s. Considering that Christian finds inspiration everywhere he goes, it's not a surprise that he wanted to try his hand at Cozy Cat's group mystery: "I loved it! I was honored to have the opportunity to write the first chapter. As each new chapter was written, and each author put his or her spin on it, deepening the suspense, action, mystery, I followed along. Wow, what a ride!" Unlike many of the authors, Christian's biggest challenge wasn't trying to match the previous author's writing style, but instead it was letting go of the story he had begun. However, starting the novel was also one of the most enjoyable parts of being included in the

mystery. "Developing an interesting story with lots of room to explore, creating a new setting, a new character, a new everything! It was fun!" Christian's experience with reading mysteries was a great help to him too: "My favorites are Sue Grafton and Michael Connelly. I also enjoy the classics such as Rex Stout and Raymond Chandler." Christian's message to readers is: "Twists and turns galore, mysteries and thrills make you wanting more. Bryn's boyfriend disappears, her niece is taken, who's being honest and who's fakin'? This roller coaster rocks, hold on tight or you may lose your socks!"

Christian is a graduate of Michigan's Lawrence Technology University, where he received a degree in architecture. He's been an architect for over 30 years, and has used his experiences and clients to help create his novels. He was born in Berlin, but grew up in East Detroit after his parents immigrated to America. One of his favorite places when he was growing up was a bakery near his house where his mother used to buy Polish rye every week.

Christian's other publications include some short stories, poems, and a chapter entitled "Persistence" in *The 28-Day Thought Diet.* In his free time, Christian enjoys ballroom dancing. To find out more about Christian and his books, visit his website at: http://kenknollmystery.com/christian-belz-more-information/

Lane Buckman is beauty queen turned writer who once believed that writing the Great American Novel was her calling. However, she quickly realized trying to write a serious novel was a little too uptight for her comedic nature. So she decided to try her hand at other types of literature. She started by co-authoring a vampire novel, then began her cozy mystery *Tiara Trouble*, and after that a romance which turned out to be a bigger success than her Great American Novel.

With all her writing experiences, it's no surprise that Lane wanted to take part in Cozy Cat's group mystery: "All writing is practice for future writing. I've learned a lot through every editorial process, and hope it has improved my work each time." Of course, it wasn't like writing her own work: "I had serious writer's block. It was not easy picking up someone else's thread and pressing forward." She pushed on: "I was the second writer, so I got to add a POV shift. I enjoyed the character, so I hope the readers do, too." Lane had a great time participating in the group mystery project: "It's like a buffet of writers. You can sample a little bit of each, decide what you like best, then go back for more!"

Lane graduated from the University of Texas at Arlington with a bachelor's degree in English Literature. When she writes, Lane writes the stories she would like to read, and the ones she's lived that she believes are worth telling. She also has a blog, and owns her own publishing imprint Robyn Lane Books.

Lane was born in North Carolina, but currently lives in Dallas, Texas. To learn more about Lane, her books, her blog, and more visit her website: lanebuckman.com

 **Sally Carpenter** enjoys writing and reading in her free time, and is currently employed at a community newspaper. However, she is anything but typical. Sally certainly hasn't had a boring life. She has been an actress with a traveling drama troupe, a jail chaplain, a college writing instructor, a

preacher, a tour guide/page for Paramount Pictures, and she has a black belt in tae kwon do.

With Sally's extensive life experiences, it's no surprise that she wanted to add writing a group mystery to her list. There were differences and difficulties she had to overcome: "Taking characters and a storyline that other people had produced and moving the story forward from there was difficult. I would have taken the story in a different direction." However, Sally still had a lot fun writing her chapter: "I enjoyed it a lot. The chapter was an assignment that I didn't have to spend the time and planning that I would for an entire book. Putting my own individual "stamp" on my chapter was enjoyable. I write retro cozies, so I created an aging hippie, a character I'm sure nobody else would have dreamed up."

Sally was born in Indiana, growing up in Princeton. Since then, she's lived in various Midwest cities. In 2000, she moved to California where she settled in Moorpark. She has a Master of Arts in theater from Indiana State University and a Master of Divinity from Garrett-Evangelical Theological Seminary. However, according to Sally, her many degrees do not mean she's mastered anything.

As well as writing and reading, Sally also enjoys watching old TV shows and movies, and listening to music from her record/CD/tape collection. Along with her mysteries, Sally has also published some short plays, as well as play reviews for a local theater. She writes the Roots of Faith column for Acorn Newspapers.

To find out more about Sally, her mysteries, and more, visit her website: http://sandyfairfaxauthor.com.

Barbara Jean Coast is a pseudonym for Cozy Cat Press authors Heather Shkuratoff and Andrea Taylor. As two authors who already enjoy writing as a team, it comes as no surprise that they wanted to write with a bigger team. "It was a great creative challenge," said Andrea. "It was neat to see how everyone had a different take on the story," said Heather. Their alter ego, Barbara Jean, also chimed in: "I have a blast no matter what I do!"

Heather and Andrea both found challenges too with the group mystery: "Accuracy and cohesiveness as the story went along was difficult. With our own mysteries, we can tell the full story, develop the characters further and have a structured plot that runs throughout the book." However, they were able to come together for the over all benefit of the story: "By the time we came to the project, we had to make decisions on how to pull the common threads out among the previous chapters and string them together to make it as cohesive as possible."

Heather and Andrea have been lifelong friends. Andrea was born in Vancouver, British Columbia, Canada, and grew up in Oliver. Heather was born and raised in Oliver. Now they both live in Kelowna, British Columbia. Both women have had numerous jobs throughout their lives which have helped them don the persona of Barbara Jean and write her Poppy Cove mysteries. Barbara Jean has her own blog: http://www.barbarajeancoast.com/, where she promotes her books, writes about what's going on in her life (along with Heather's and Andrea's too), and keeps her readers updated on events, appearances and other things related to her Poppy Cove mysteries.

 **Bart J. Gilbertson** is a humble mystery writer who likes to remind others that authors should write simply because they love to write. Bart discovered his own love of reading in the fourth grade because of his teacher, Mrs. Parks, who read to the class every day after recess. In junior high, Bart took his first gamble at writing and brought his work back to his old teacher for feedback. Mrs. Parks did more than just give feedback; she read his work to her class. From that day on, Bart knew he wanted to become an author, and years later, through Cozy Cat Press, Bart published his first mystery.

Bart says: "I really enjoyed doing my part for the group mystery. It's a lot of fun to be involved with a project where you get to contribute to the overall voice of the novel." It was also a great learning experience, he says, "Granted, the more you write, the better you become. But this project was so different from anything I've ever done before. I just wanted my chapter to resonate well with the rest of the book. I hope I've done it justice." Of course, Bart brought his own techniques to writing his chapter: "I shut out everything else in my life when I write. I become my characters. I try to bring them to life as if they were sitting right there next to me. That's my goal, to make them real."

Bart was born in Rhinelander, Wisconsin, but he spent most of his youth in northern Idaho in the Moscow-Troy area. He's traveled all over the northwestern United States, and is currently living in

O'Neill, Nebraska. He fell in love with a town called Sisters in Oregon, and used it as inspiration for the setting of his mystery. A graduate of ITT Technical Institute, where he received an Associate's degree in Applied Science for Computing Networking Systems, Bart graduated with honors. Bart also has a website at http://bjgilbertson2.wix.com/bartjgilbertson.   Here readers can find information about his books, his blog, and other events.

Helen Grochmal's writing career began when she wrote her first two mysteries while she was living in a senior living center. Since then, she's written a memoir, numerous short stories, and library articles for library journals. Helen believes her first career as a customs inspector should have helped her write mysteries, but she says, "Everyone's story was believable to me. 'So that's why your two sets of receipts don't match? Oh, yes, of course! I see the reason. How foolish of me to ask'." Perhaps, it was her twenty years as a librarian that inspired her writing, along with fifty years of reading mysteries.

The decision to help write Cozy Cat's group mystery came at a good time when her inspiration was high— and not held captive by a writer's sworn enemy: writer's block. Being part of the group mystery was important to Helen: "The most enjoyable part of it was feeling like part of a fun group with a task to do. I don't leave my apartment much so it meant more to *me* than to anyone else, I would imagine." She says, "I read the earlier chapters and then started to write down as quickly as I could what my mind was dictating to me. It was all fun, although I was afraid at times that I was taking too much of a departure in the plot, but I had to trust my gift. My conservative mind told me the plot was still in the early stages so it could handle two new characters. They could have been killed off early if someone later didn't like them." Of course, there were difficulties: "Seeing my own innocent but smart characters of whom I had grown quite fond seen in a different way by others was the hardest. But, of course, that's part of the fun of a group mystery."

In her free time, Helen enjoys reading and watching TV—a pastime that she says is a godsend for her fellow residents in her senior community in Rockville, Maryland. She was born in Wilkes-Barre, Pennsylvania, where she lived until the age of 23. She is a graduate of Wilkes University where she earned her bachelor's degree in English. She received a Master's in English from Pennsylvania State University, and a M.L.S. in Library Service from Rutgers University.

 **Tim Hall** says that his day jobs are the reason he's able to write at all. Tim has had a lot of temporary jobs, but eventually he began a career as a production artist, doing graphics for a financial firm. Tim's writing career truly began when he received his first health insurance card, and he finally felt like his life was stable enough to spend time writing. His writing has appeared in THUGLIT, *BIGnews*, and *Chicago Reader*, and he will soon have a story featured in *Cannibal Cookbook Anthology*. Tim himself appears at numerous events throughout the year, such as Malice Domestic, Deadly Ink, Noir at the Bar, BEA, KGB reading series, and the Brooklyn Book Festival.

Tim is active in the writing world and enjoyed being part of Cozy Cat's collaboration. "I'm always in my own head, otherwise, which is not a very nice place to be sometimes." Of the challenges, he says: "Trying to follow the first drafts of all these chapters and find a way to keep the story moving in a meaningful way was hard." However, overall, the experience of being a part of the group mystery was one of a kind for Tim: "I loved it! It was completely bonkers and improbable and I can't imagine it could possibly all hold together—but knowing Patricia Rockwell and her genius for making things happen, I bet it will be wonderful!" Tim's message to readers is: "You will automatically lose twenty pounds if you read it. Guaranteed."

Tim originally attended the University of Chicago, but was unable to graduate. However, after his son was born, Tim went back to school and graduated from DePaul University in 2013, with a degree in Multimedia Writing and Communications.

In his free time Tim enjoy cooking, watching movies, and listening to music. Visit Tim's website at https://timhallbooks.wordpress.com/ where you can learn more about Tim, his mysteries, and more.

Owen Magruder claims that his inspiration for writing mysteries came from Sir Arthur Doyle and his Sherlock Holmes novels. Since then, Owen has used his travels to Nova Scotia, Scotland, and England, along with living in an American college town to inspire his writing. He believes that writing is more joyous without using a detailed outline. He likes to give his characters the freedom to decide where they want to go.

Participating in the Cozy Cat group mystery wasn't the first time Owen has helped write one: "My first experience was in a bed and breakfast in New Mexico. In the guest book, each visitor was asked to add to an ongoing story about the Southwest. I have never seen the completed work—if it ever was completed." Owen found writing the group mystery an interesting experience: "The give and take of blending differing ideas is always good preparation for group writing, though with the Cozy Cat manuscript, there was no direct interaction among the authors." Despite his one previous group writing experience, Owen still experienced difficulties: "My mysteries are very carefully crafted and tightly written. Achieving that with a group of authors can be problematic. It will depend on the final editor as to how cohesive the final product is." However, he tried to "make my contribution carry forward logically what had gone before and yet leave several paths for the next author to pursue."

Owen has lived in many places throughout his life. He was born and raised in Baltimore, where he spent his first twenty years. He then joined the army for two years, and was sent to Korea for ten months. He spent two years living in Tuscaloosa, Alabama, four years living in Lexington, Kentucky, and four years living in St. Louis, Missouri (site of the group mystery's notorious book convention!). He currently lives in Hamilton, New York. Owen received a Bachelor's degree from Johns Hopkins University, a Master's from the University of Alabama, and a Ph.D. from the University of Kentucky. He has been a professor at four different colleges, and has many publications outside of his mysteries. In his free time, Owen enjoys oil painting, writing, and reading.

Joyce Oroz is a writer who likes to be outside each day enjoying the fresh air. She spends a lot of time in her garden, and draws inspiration from the beauty of her home in California, which is why she's never felt the need to live anywhere but California. Writing was the second art form Joyce tried, having first discovered the arts as a mural painter. For 28 years, Joyce painted murals in homes and businesses. Unfortunately, standing on a ladder for long periods of time became too strenuous, and so she went from painter to writer. Since then, she's written 27 children's books, and seven books in her Josephine Stuart mystery series. According to Joyce, "Writing is like painting but without the mess."

Of the group mystery, Joyce says, "I enjoyed the process, watching what other writers wrote, hoping the story would come together at the end. We writers all have vivid imaginations. It was fun reading the chapters as they appeared, one by one, full of adventure and mystery." It was challenging to be in charge of one chapter—and one chapter only. "It wasn't easy staying on-track with the original characters and storyline, as I tried to push the story forward." However, Joyce persevered. "I write mysteries, so I did what I always do. I stared at my computer and hoped the right words would come to me. It's always fun and exciting when the ideas show themselves." Joyce's message to readers of the group mystery is simple and straightforward: "Try it—you'll like it."

Joyce was born and raised in California. She's studied art and English throughout her lifetime. With every book she writes, she tries to improve her writing. Joyce has a blog: http://authorjoyceoroz.blogspot.com, where she writes about various experiences, topics, and tries to give advice to other writers who might be reading.

Emma Pivato's life experiences have taken her down some different paths. When her daughter was diagnosed with developmental disabilities, Emma trained to become an assessment psychologist, and this experience later provided her with the background for her mysteries. She has traveled a lot, but Mexico left a distinct impression on her, and she used some of her experiences from those travels in her book *Roscoe's Revenge.* She has also used settings from Barbados and the Bahamas in two of her other books.

Emma was thrilled to have the opportunity to participate in Cozy Cat Press's group mystery. "It was a real privilege to be part of this, to see how other people write and to try to put myself in their mind-set and writing style so the work would flow. I liked it a lot!" Emma found similarities between writing the group mystery and writing her own books: "We were all trying to set up red herrings and then work towards a satisfying resolution." She found that the difficult and enjoyable parts often overlapped: "It was a challenge to fit in what I had to say in such a way that it would not close off too many options for the writers who wrote after me. It was intriguing to follow the twists and turns and to see where others' imaginations and writing styles took them!" Emma would like readers to know that, "Reading this group mystery is a good way to dip one's toe into the world of mystery writing and see how different writers set up different situations. Readers can discover that there is a structured process behind this particular art form."

Emma is a graduate of the University of Alberta, where she received a Bachelor's degree in psychology and philosophy, a Master's degree in philosophy, and a Ph.D. in educational psychology. Emma has also done a lot of work advocating for individuals born with developmental disabilities. She is the developer of GRIT, an in home/in community program for preschoolers with severe disabilities. She's also written a book entitled *Different Hopes, Different Dreams,* which is a collection of essays from parents of children with development disabilities. She has been working on building a specialized wheelchair for disabled children like her daughter. She's still working out the kinks, but has a model and patent.

Drema Reed is an author whose writing career took off after she retired from life-long work in the medical field. She's used her home town of Seattle, and her travels to the Middle East to inspire her mysteries and her "Books of the Dead" series of adventure/mystery/romance novels. Since launching her writing career, Drema has published three books in her "Art Gallery" mystery series with Cozy Cat Press.

Drema states that, "Writing the group mystery was fun. I would love to do it again." In fact, any difficulties that occurred during the process were acceptable to her: "I enjoyed reading what the other authors in the group wrote and seeing their different styles." Drema made sure to add her own unique charm to the mystery: "I used humor to lighten up an otherwise serious book." Drema would like readers to know that writing the group mystery, "was sort of like herding cats!"

Drema is a graduate of California State University, Pierce Junior College of Nursing, and Portland State

University, where she received a Bachelors' degree in anthropology this past June, and where she was also honored for being the oldest graduate of the school.

Drema has just started her own publishing company entitled Celtic House Press. She was born in Charleston, West Virginia, but grew up in California. She now lives in Oregon.

 **Joe and Pam (T'Gracie) Reese** are writers whose joint mystery career took off in 2012. Before then, Joe had published two novels, along with having had several of his plays performed. For years, Pam had begged Joe to write a mystery, and it wasn't until they were inspired by a stop in Bay St. Louis, Mississippi, that Pam and Joe started to plan out their first cozy mystery, *Sea Change*. Since the publication of that book, they've written six additional mysteries with Cozy Cat Press—all drawing from real life places and experiences. As their mystery writing career has been booming, it's no surprise that they wanted to try their hand at writing with a group. "We found writing the group mystery an intriguing challenge, never having written this way before." However, even with their experience at writing together, there were still problems: "By the time we got the story, we felt there was not a strong sense of place. In the story, Bryn and her friends seemed to be going many places and experiencing many dangerous and exciting adventures. However, a true cozy mystery is usually rooted in a small town or village. We hadn't gotten a sense of such a place when it came time for us to make our contribution." Another challenge was trying to give the novel a sense of direction: "Joe particularly tried to go heavily on description,

memories and a sense of Bryn's past. Reading all of the plot twists made it difficult to know what we should add, but that was also probably the most enjoyable part." Joe and Pam's message to readers is this: "Fans of cozy mysteries should be delighted to read a book co-written by some of the best cozy mystery writers around—each one adding new and exciting characters, locales and surprising plot twists."

Joe is a graduate of Southern Methodist University, where he received his Bachelor's degree; Tulane University, where he received his Master's degree; and Indiana University, where he received his Ph.D. Pam is a graduate of Southern Methodist University, where she received her Bachelor's degree; Indiana University, where she received her M.A.T.; and the University of Louisiana-Lafayette, where she received her Ph.D.

If you want to learn more about Joe and Pam you can visit their website: http://ninabannister.com/about-the-authors/

 **Patricia Rockwell** is the author of two mystery series. Her Pamela Barnes acoustic mysteries include *Sounds of Murder, FM For Murder, Voice Mail Murder, Stump Speech Murder,* and *Murder in the Round.* Her Essie Cobb senior sleuth mysteries include *Bingoed, Papoosed, Valentined,* and *Ghosted.* She is the founder and publisher of Cozy Cat Press, which specializes in producing cozy (or gentle) mysteries.

Patricia concocted the idea of the group mystery because she wanted to utilize the talents of her many authors in a new way. She had not really planned to write a chapter herself, but decided to include one when she discovered some "plot holes" along the way. "I realized as we went along that there were a number of unexplained issues for the main character, Bryn, mostly dealing with the history of her bookstore and how and why she was involved in the search for the strange bible and the code. I created Elena, the previous owner of the bookstore, and the relationship between the two women. I added a short chapter where they communicate by phone. Other than this brief interlude, I tried to stay out of the story." Patricia hopes that readers enjoy the group mystery as it was intended—an exciting, engaging experience. She also hopes that readers will use the group mystery to find new authors they might enjoy reading.

Patricia has Bachelors' and Masters' degrees from the University of Nebraska in Speech, and a Ph.D. from the University of Arizona in Communication. She was on the faculty at the University of Louisiana at Lafayette for thirteen years, retiring in 2007. Her publications are extensive, with over 20 peer-reviewed articles in scholarly journals, several textbooks, and a research book on her major interest area of sarcasm, published by Edwin Mellen Press. In addition to writing and publishing her own academic research, she also served for eight years as editor of the *Louisiana Communication Journal*. Her research focuses primarily on deception, sarcasm, and vocal cues.

Dr. Rockwell is presently living in Aurora, Illinois, with her husband Milt, also a retired educator. Visit her website at: www.patriciarockwellauthor.com.

 **Sharon Rose** is a writer who let the time for writing come to her, instead of the other way around. She waited until all four of her children were grown and out of the house before she deemed the time suitable for pursuing the ideas she'd stored up inside her for

so long. To start, Sharon enrolled in a three-year writing program, after which she sold her first short story—which happened to contain the two main characters in her Parson's Cove mystery series: Mabel Wickles and Flori Flanders. Since then, she's written numerous short stories and novels.

When it came time to decide whether or not to participate in the group mystery, Sharon decided that the time was right: "Perhaps having written several cozy mysteries, it's quite easy to ease yourself into another one. Reading everyone's different writing styles was enjoyable. It seemed to bring out their own personalities and added a bit of flair to the story." Of course, there were challenges: "I was told I would write a certain chapter, but I had no idea what the book was even about!" However, Sharon rose to the challenge: "When it came my turn, I had no problem blending in. It seems most of the Cozy Cat writers have a similar way of writing. My cozies are more on the humorous side, but that would be the only difference." Sharon adds: "With our group mystery, the writers themselves didn't know how it would end. If they couldn't know, I challenge any reader to figure it out!"

Sharon spent her life growing up in small towns, which is where she gets a lot of her inspiration. Small towns are comfortable and she feels the most relaxed when creating settings in small towns. While Sharon had a variety of jobs throughout her life, she doesn't feel as if they influenced her writing. Instead, she states, her mother is the main reason she became a writer, as her mother was both a writer and a poet.

Readers can visit Sharon's website at http://sharonrosemierke.weebly.com where she promotes herself, her books, her Twitter and Facebook pages, Cozy Cat Press, and other cozy mysteries.

 **Julie Seedorf** has taken many different paths in life. She's been a computer technician, a waitress, a worker in a nursing home, a bartender, an administrative assistant, a volunteer coordinator, and a computer business owner. However, her most important career has been motherhood. All of Julie's experiences and the places she's travelled have inspired her, because she sees mystery everywhere she goes. Even the small community in Minnesota where she's lived her whole life has provided inspiration.

Since Julie loves to get her hands into everything, it's no surprise that she joined the group mystery. She says the best part was, "connecting with the other writers and seeing where their imaginations led them." She claims it was difficult trying to align her part of the mystery with the rest of the plot, with all those "events you don't expect." Julie would like readers to know that, "This mystery, written by talented Cozy Cat Press writers, is filled with twists and turns, surprising even the writers—creative minds working together for murder and mayhem."

Julie writes a weekly column for her hometown newspaper in Albert Lea, Minnesota, called, "Something About Nothing," and has also published a book of her columns. She writes a children's series entitled, "The Granny's in Trouble." Julie freelances for several newspapers, and has written a book called, *We Go On: A Charity Anthology for Veterans,* in which the proceeds go to various veterans' programs. In her free time, Julie enjoys learning new arts such as painting, stained glass, and repurposing furniture. And, there are still more things Julie would love to learn.

Julie has two websites: http://julieseedorf.com and http://sprinklednotes.com. At SprinkedNotes, there is a blog, which includes articles she wrote for the *Courier Sentinel*, descriptions of her favorite things, and much more.

 **David Selcer** is a writer who uses his law experience to make his books come to life. David worked in a national law firm for 35 years and, during that time, argued many different cases in many different court rooms. He wrote briefs for and argued in courts of appeals as well. With his dedication to the law, it's no surprise that David's mysteries have a legal angle. So far, he's published three books in his Buckeye Barrister series and he's working on his fourth. On the side, David also writes EEO decisions for various federal agencies.

When the opportunity to branch out occurred, David jumped at the chance to be a part of Cozy Cat Press's group mystery. "It was a different sort of challenge to write something to fit what somebody else wrote, but not as much as writing an entire book," he says. However, David used his own strengths to figure out a way to write his chapter: "I didn't think the group mystery was funny enough. I enjoy injecting humor when I write." He also likes writing dialogue. Regarding the group mystery, he tells mystery buffs to, "Read it and try to figure out connections between the background of each writer and the chapter h/she wrote."

David is a graduate of Northwestern University where he received a Bachelor's degree in History, and of the College of Law at Ohio State University. While his books are inspired by his law career, he also draws inspiration from his love for the city of Colombus, and the state of Ohio. David was born in Cleveland, but grew up Wooster, Ohio. Now he splits his time between living in Columbus, and in Sarasota, Florida. He has also traveled to Belgium and Israel, and has occasionally used those locations as locales in his books.

David has raised five children with his wife, and enjoys fishing in his free time.

 **Steve Shrott** is a writer who considers his work time the same as his free time. The things he does in his free time such as write, perform and teach comedy, as well as create magic, are the same things he does for his day jobs. Reading, watching movies, and walking around bookstores are also things Steve likes to do.

Since Steve loves to seek out new things to experience, he was happy to volunteer for Cozy Cat's group mystery: "It was a lot of fun being involved. My mysteries are pretty much straight humor, while the group mystery is a mix of humor and suspense, drama, etc." Steve's writing experiences assisted him in putting his mark on the group mystery: "I think the fact that I had written lots of short stories helped me to write my section of it. The enjoyable part was that the characters were already established. So I just had to write another story about them. I also enjoyed trying to figure out what my story would be about," Steve says. "This is a fun and exciting book as well as unique, since a different writer wrote each chapter. It'll give you an opportunity to sample each writer's work"

Steve was born and raised in Toronto, Canada, where he lives today. He's a graduate of York University where he received a Bachelor of Arts and a teaching degree. He draws a lot of inspiration from California, where he's spent a lot of time. For Steve,

California is where the greatest detective novels and movies have taken place. In addition to his Cozy Cat Press mysteries, he's also written a book on how to write comedy, along with some short mystery stories published in magazines, ezines, and anthologies.

Steve invites readers to visit his website: http://steveshrottwriter.weebly.com where he has information on each of his career pursuits.

 **Leslie Matthews Stansfield** is a private but dedicated writer. She's written two mysteries so far in her Madeline's Teahouse mystery series: *Mr. Tea and the Traveling Teacup* and *Mr. Tea and the Bobbin' Body.* She has also written a novel called *Windsor Locks,* which is a book about the town she lives in. Leslie gives credit to her friends for helping develop her imagination.

It's no surprise that Leslie participated in Cozy Cat's group mystery, as it was a way for her to use her imagination.

Not only is Leslie dedicated to her writing, but she also is dedicated to helping children and their education. She tutors students in math at a public school, as well as being the Christian Education Director of her church.

Leslie is a graduate of the University of Hartford, and recently received a Master's degree in Educational Leadership from the University of Phoenix. Leslie grew up in Delmar, New York, and currently lives in Windsor Locks, Connecticut. She has four children and eight grandchildren.

Lane Stone is a writer whose first job at Six Flags Over Georgia helped instill in her a strong work ethic that to this day keeps her writing on track. So far, Lane has produced two novels of her own, *Current Affairs* and *Domestic Affairs;* a co-authored novel, *Maltipoos Are Murder;* and, of course, this group mystery.

Lane was enthused about the opportunity to participate in the group mystery: "My specialty is writing humor, but I had to rein that in for my chapter, to blend in with what had already been written. The voice had to be the same." She says, "This protagonist is such a nice person. In my books, the dialog has a lot of irony and sarcasm. And I have co-protagonists in my series. In the group mystery, the main character has a good supporting cast, but basically solving the mystery is on her shoulders." Lane was still able to put her personal touch on the group mystery: "My previous work taught me how to recognize good, solid plotting. The Cozy Cat authors are such great writers. I loved doing it, and I can't wait to read the finished product!" Lane tells readers that with the group mystery, "We're carrying on a time-honored tradition in the mystery world. The Detection Club, with members such as Agatha Christie and Dorothy L. Sayers, published several mysteries written by multiple authors, with each author writing a chapter or two."

Lane was born and raised in Georgia, where she gets a lot of her inspiration. According to her, Georgians commit the best crimes, and are funny and witty: "For example," she says, "one Georgia woman poisoned her husband, along with her lover's wife. The judge asked her why she didn't just get a divorce. The woman answered, 'Divorce is too hard on young children.'"

Lane also does a lot of volunteer work. She's on the Georgia State Political Science Advisory Board. She's the Campus Outreach Coordinator for the Alexandria Branch of AAUW—American Association for University Women. She's also a member of JASNA, the Jane Austen Society of North America. Lane enjoys playing golf in her free time, and she's learning to play bridge.

You can learn more about Lane at her website: www.lanestonebooks.com.

 **Jennifer Vido** began her career as a French teacher. However, fate soon led her into the writing world. Her publishing career started with a "Reading with Ripa" roundtable discussion with Kelly Ripa and Meg Cabot. She is currently the book editor at www.momtrends.com, the author of the Piper O'Donnell mystery series, and a reviewer of various book genres and exercise videos. She also keeps busy with book signings and tours.

Jennifer signed on to help write Cozy Cat's group mystery, viewing it as an opportunity to improve her writing skills. "Writing a group mystery was much different than writing my own novel," she says, "because I had ownership of only a small part of the project. It was a collaborative process and. I thoroughly enjoyed it." Jennifer brought her own special skills to the group: "As a book reviewer, I was familiar with the key elements needed for a book's success in the publishing business. I was able to put to good use my knowledge of sequencing from my three previous novels in order to help construct the flow of the story." She particularly enjoyed reading the chapters in the group mystery following her own as they were produced. She says, "The Cozy Cat Press group mystery best exemplifies the many talents of our writers."

Along with being an editor, reviewer, and author, Jennifer also serves on the National Board of the Arthritis Foundation. As someone who suffers from the nation's number one cause of disability, she is determined to get the word out about this disease. She's a national spokesperson for the Arthritis Foundation, and is a national trainer for their Aquatic and Land Exercise classes.

Jennifer was born in northern New Jersey, and her childhood was spent on the Jersey shore. She now lives in the Baltimore area with her husband and two teenage sons, where she enjoys reading romance and mystery novels, as well as watching reality shows on Bravo television. She graduated from Vanderbilt University with a B.S. in French and Secondary Education.

You can find out more about Jennifer, her books, and more at her website: www.JenniferVido.com

 **Diane Weiner** is an active writer who loves to create worlds where she herself would love to be, or that are based on places she's been. Diane hasn't always been a writer. She went to college and graduated as a music major, taught in the public schools for 26 years, and even was a music teacher for five years at the American School in Mexico City. She also served for a time as a principal at a private school. She likes to run, work out, shop, and attend community theater productions.

Diane noted some major differences between writing her own books and writing a chapter for the group mystery: "I have an outline for my own books and

know where the story is heading. I didn't have such an overview for the group mystery. The most difficult thing was making a smooth transition from what came before." However, that didn't take away from the experience for her: "I enjoyed writing my chapter." Diane's message to readers is: "The group mystery has a little bit of everything you'd expect to see in a mystery—a secret room, code in a bible, evil twins..."

Diane is an animal lover, which is one of the reasons she became a vegetarian. She's a mother of four, and has two cats and a dog. She loves to spend time with her family, go to the mall with her daughter and get Dairy Queen. Diane is a graduate of University of North Carolina-Chapel Hill, Nova Southeastern, and Walden University. She was born in Teaneck, New Jersey, grew up in Highland, New York, and now lives in Coral Springs, Florida.

Diane doesn't have a website, but she does have an author page on amazon.com and Goodreads.

* * * * *

Cozy Cat Press is a small, independent publisher of cozy (or "gentle") mysteries based in Aurora, IL. The company was founded in 2010 by Patricia Rockwell and today includes over 40 authors and 100 titles. Our books are available in both print and e-book versions at amazon.com. If you enjoyed this book, please consider posting a review on your favorite retailer's website. For more information about Cozy Cat Press, visit our website at: www.cozycatpress.com

COZY CAT
PRESS

Made in the USA
Lexington, KY
13 August 2017